A Five-Dollar Bet

"At this time tomorrow," I said, in my most important and quiet voice, "if Goldie's dead, I'm going to swallow the goldfish."

"Big deal," said Bailey. "Big freakin' deal."

And then she did several things practically at the same time: She leaned back, took something out of her pocket, and smacked it down on the desk she was sitting on. "Five bucks."

"Five bucks what?" Brant piped up.

"Five bucks if Big Shot there not only swallows the goldfish." She squinted up her eyes at me. "You gotta chew it, Big Shot."

Kevin Corbett Eats Flies

by PATRICIA HERMES

illustrated by
CAROL NEWSOM

A
MINSTREL™
BOOK

PUBLISHED BY POCKET BOOKS

A Minstrel Book published by
POCKET BOOKS, a division of Simon & Schuster, Inc.,
1230 Avenue of the Americas, New York, N.Y. 10020

Text copyright © 1986 by Patricia Hermes
Illustrations copyright © 1986 by Carol Newsom

Published by arrangement with Harcourt Brace Jovanovich, Inc.
Library of Congress Catalog Card Number: 85-27086

ISBN: 0-671-63790-8

First Minstrel Books printing December, 1987

10 9 8 7 6 5 4 3 2 1

A MINSTREL BOOK and colophon are trademarks
of Simon & Schuster, Inc.

Printed in the U.S.A.

With love I dedicate this book to my daughter Jennifer Hermes because without Jennifer this book would not have come into being. The idea, the poetry, and any laughter that may be in this book are Jennifer's gift to me.

And so Jennifer for you, with love and gratitude.

ACKNOWLEDGMENT: All the poems in this book were written by Jennifer Hermes.

List of Illustrations

Kevin Corbett
Eats Flies

1

IT WAS TIME. It was definitely time. The morning had been so boring that I had already written two poems in my head, and I couldn't wait to get them written down. But for right then, I had something much more important to do, and Miss Holt had finally left the classroom. She had taken her thermos of coffee with her, too, so that meant she'd be across the hall for fifteen minutes at least, with Mrs. Gillespie, the other fifth-grade teacher. Plenty of time.

I stood up, and then very slowly walked to the front of the room and peered into the fish tank. Goldie, the half-dead goldfish, was there at the surface of the water, its mouth opening and closing, gasping for air.

"Poor thing. Almost dead," I said loudly. I was talking to everybody, but I looked right at Janie, who had been left in charge of the class.

Brant, my best friend, says that Janie's in love with me. I think he's full of it. But just in case, I smiled at Janie, trying to soften her up so she wouldn't tell on me.

Her face got all red, and she looked away.

"And know what's going to happen when he dies?" I asked the class in general.

1

"What?" Brant piped up.

Brant's a little kid, about a foot shorter than anyone else in the class, with eyes that are bigger than anyone's I've ever seen. And he's my best friend. It's hard to have a best friend when you move around about every six months the way I do, but Brant and I have been friends ever since I moved to Stamford last April—six whole months already.

"So what's going to happen?" he asked again.

"Well. . . ."

I looked around and saw that I had everybody's attention, all but the new kid, Bailey, and a few kids near her who were watching her expectantly. She was leaning back in her chair chewing gum, and she had just blown a bubble so big that it hid her entire little face and straggly brown hair.

I waited for the bubble to pop, and when it did, I looked directly at her.

"You!" I pointed a finger at her the way Miss Mitchell, our fourth-grade teacher, used to do when she thought she'd catch you without the right answer. "Want to guess what's going to happen when Goldie dies?"

Her eyes were crossed as she concentrated on picking bubble gum strands off her nose.

Three seconds. Four seconds. Five.

Then, still looking at her nose, she said, "You talking to me?"

"Yeah."

"My name's Bailey." Her voice was funny, deep and rough, like a pebble being scuffed across a sidewalk.

"Oh." I was embarrassed, and to cover up, I began fiddling with the dials of the complicated calendar watch

Pop had just given me. I guessed it wasn't real polite to call her "you," but how come Miss Mitchell had always gotten away with it?

"So," I said, looking up from the watch. "Want to guess what's going to happen when Goldie dies?"

Bailey picked another strand of gum off her nose, put the gum in her mouth, and stood up. She came to the front of the room and stood next to me. With a quick movement, she dipped her hand into the fishbowl and scooped Goldie out. She held him up before her eyes, squinting, and then put him carefully, almost gently, back in the bowl.

"It'll be dead by morning," she said to everybody, and went back to her place. She sat down on top of her desk, swinging her legs. She looked right at me, as if daring me to do something.

"Right!" I said. And then for the fourth time I said, "And know what happens when he dies?"

Bailey rolled her eyes up, and put her hands on her hips—if you could call them that—jutting little shelves of bone. "I suppose," she said to the ceiling, "I suppose he thinks it's going to fish heaven."

"Yeah, Kevin, is that what you think?"

Everybody was talking at once.

I didn't even bother to glare at them. I just gave them my "You're such *children*" look, and waited for them to quiet down. I looked at Brant. He was posted at the door, watching out for Miss Holt's return. He gave me the sign that it was still okay.

When everybody finally quieted down, I held up my wrist and looked carefully at my watch. "At this time to-morrow," I said, in my most important and quiet voice, "if Goldie's dead, and as soon as I'm sure Holt is gone—I'm going to swallow the goldfish."

There! It happened. Everybody talking at once, all excited, watching me.

"Yuck!"

"Gross!"

"Really? Are you really?"

"You're nuts!"

They were all staring at me. Even Bailey was watching me thoughtfully.

"Oooh, but you'll get sick!" Janie squeaked.

I gave her a *look*. But I supposed that's what I got for smiling at her before.

"You really going to do it?" Brant's big eyes were even wider.

"Yup."

Through all the noise and squealing came a pop—a crack like something chomping concrete. Bailey, popping another bubble. It stopped everybody. "Big deal," she said. "Big freakin' deal."

And then she did several things practically at the same time: she leaned back, took something out of her pocket, and smacked it down on the desk that she was sitting on.

"Five bucks." She said it sort of carelessly, and she didn't look at me anymore. Her head was bent as if she was talking to her sneakers.

Everybody waited.

She didn't speak again.

"Five bucks, what?" Brant piped up.

Good old Brant.

Bailey was still looking at her sneakers. "Five bucks because anyone can swallow a goldfish. People have been

4

swallowing goldfish for years. Don't any of you even *read*? It's history, folks." She looked up then and right at me. "But I have five bucks if Big Shot there not only swallows the goldfish." She squinted up her eyes at me. "You gotta chew it, Big Shot."

"My name's Kevin," I said. But my voice came out odd and a little squeaky.

This time there was even more squealing than before, and I was sure that Holt would hear us and come racing back in, wanting to know what was going on. Janie wasn't doing a thing to stop it. She had a hand over her mouth, and she looked sick.

"Will you shush up?" I said. "You'll all be in trouble. Me, too. You want extra homework?"

I glared at them angrily, as if that's what I was thinking about, but a voice in my head kept saying, "Chew it? *Chew* it?"

They got more quiet, but were still making squeaking, squealing noises like somebody had let loose about a hundred mice in the room. And all of them were watching me, waiting. All but Bailey. She acted like she didn't notice or care that there was this big uproar. She was calmly chewing on her fingernails.

"Don't do it, Kevin," Brant said. "Are you going to do it? Don't do it."

Again, everybody started. "Are you? Are you?"

But not Bailey. She didn't say a word. She was still nibbling on her fingernails, but I thought I could see her smiling behind her little paw.

"Yeah, I'll do it!" I said. "And shut up!" I added quickly, before they could all start squeaking again.

"Hey, Bailey!" Brant took a step away from the door

and toward Bailey. "Bailey?" he said quietly. "How about letting him wrap it in paper first, okay?"

She tilted her head to one side so that her straggly hair fell half over one eye. With the uncovered eye, she looked at Brant. "Okay," she said. "That's fair."

The eye looked at me. "But after a few bites you gotta open your mouth so we can see you really did it. That you didn't just make faces like you were chewing."

"It's cool," I said.

I stuck my hands deep in the pockets of my jeans then, and went really slowly and casually back to my desk and sat down.

This was the second time Bailey had done something rotten to me. There's this deal we have in class, that anyone who finds a dead fly gives it to me, and for five cents, I'll swallow it—ten cents for spiders, but they're harder to find. Yesterday, when Holt left for her morning coffee, and I was going to swallow two flies that Brant had brought for me, Bailey had everybody gathered around her by the windowsill so there was hardly anyone left to notice what I was doing. There were a couple of half-dead flies staggering around on the windowsill, and with a rubber band, Bailey was snapping them right off and into the air. I've never seen such an aim. And now the goldfish.

Now what? I thought. Now what? Then I thought about Pop, and I could just picture what he'd say. He'd grin and punch my shoulder. "You show 'em, son. You show 'em who's who."

Sure. I'll probably show them somebody throwing up.

But suddenly I cheered up because I had a thought. After all, nobody could be sure that Goldie would be dead by tomorrow. Sure, maybe by tomorrow, he'd be swimming around just fine. And tonight I'd talk to Pop. He might even have some ideas for how to keep a goldfish alive.

2

WHEN I GOT HOME that day, Pop was already there, sitting at the kitchen table, bent over the road atlas. . . . Oh, no! The atlas . . . maps . . . covered with coffee cup rings and ketchup stains and grease from the car. Maps. We weren't going to move again, were we? Eleven schools in six years if you counted kindergarten. That same old knotted feeling was back, like a fist in my stomach.

"Pop?" I tried to keep my voice plain, ordinary.

Pop looked up at me, a wide grin on his face. "Hey, son, lookit this." His stubby, paint-stained finger trailed across the map, fingering a thin blue line like a vein. "Oklahoma. We never been to Oklahoma. A guy I was working with today was telling me there's lots of work in Oklahoma, outdoors work, the kind I like. I wouldn't have to be cooped up doing inside painting all day. Could paint barns, things like that. And you know what else? Prairies, he says. Wide open spaces like you never seen before. Even better than that time we were in South Dakota. We could see it all together."

He was going on, praises of a new place that I bet

Pop was already there, sitting at the kitchen table, bent over the road atlas.

would turn out just like the old one. And then we'd move again.

"And you know what else, son?"

"What?"

"Maybe we'll treat ourselves to a new car, huh? You know, not brand-new. That's a waste, anyway. Drive it out of the showroom, and right away you lose all the . . . the. . . ." He looked up at me. "What's that called?"

"Equity?" I guessed. I knew what he meant—something about value. Pop's always asking me questions like that, about words and stuff. He never finished school, so he always thinks I know more about books and words than he does. But he's plenty smart about other things.

"Yeah," he said. "Equity. No, no. . . . Well, anyway, you lose all that."

He bent over the map. "Now listen to this. Right about here there's this road that goes through a prairie. . . ." His voice trailed off.

Yeah, Pop. One more place to look for something. But what? Whatever made him keep on moving. But I guess he never found it, because we always moved again.

He turned his face up to me again. And then, just like that, he closed the atlas, reached up and grabbed my belt, and tugged me down into the chair alongside him. "What's the matter? Something happen at school today? Tell the old man."

"Nothing." I couldn't tell him. The whole thing with Bailey and the goldfish and the flies. Sure, something happened. And another day I would have told him. But now it didn't seem to matter. Nothing mattered, now that he was talking about moving again.

"Come on. Something?" he said.

"No. Hey!"

He cocked his head, squinted at me, then smiled, that slow, thoughtful smile he has. His face is brown and earth-hard, and it's like watching the faces carved in rock—those presidents' faces we saw out in Mount Rushmore—like seeing one of those break into a smile. And so, of course, I couldn't help smiling back.

His dark hair had fallen over his forehead, and as he pushed it back with one hand, his blue eyes seemed to smile at me, too. People say we look alike. "Know what?" he said. "Maybe we'll wait a little while. Maybe a month or so, huh?"

"Sure." I wondered why he said that. Did he know I didn't want to leave?

"Okay," he said. "But before winter comes, we'll be on the road. And I'll be looking for a new car first."

"Okay," I said.

"So, who makes supper tonight?" he asked. He was still watching me.

"I guess it's my turn." It was hard to keep track because half the nights we went out for hamburgers or sent out for pizza, or else just ate sandwiches. I don't mind making supper, though. In fact, I'm pretty good at it, better than Pop. He knows only two dishes. One is something he calls Camp Stew. That's a can of Dinty Moore's Beef Stew, put together with whatever's left over in the refrigerator—a McDonald's hamburger that we didn't eat, or some leftover chicken that we got at a takeout place, or some beans. It's usually awful. But the other one's even worse. He calls it Egg Pizza. He scrambles up eggs, puts them in a round pan with lots of cheese on top, and then piles on tomatoes or sausages or whatever else is around.

It should taste good since I like each individual thing, but all together, it's gross.

"Well, you look in the icebox and decide," Pop said. (He still calls a refrigerator an icebox no matter how many times I've told him.) "And if you need anything else," he went on, "you can go to the store and get it." He stuck his fist in his pocket and came up with a few crumpled-up dollar bills.

I held out my hand and he put the money in it, then held my hand for a minute before he took his away. Then he opened the atlas again.

I went to my room and dumped my books, but before I went to the kitchen to decide on supper, I had something to do. I opened my desk and took out the lined notebook that I write my poems in. Two poems had come to me in class, and already one of them had escaped. I'd have to try and get it back. But I remembered one, and I wrote it down:

> In my hand I have a box,
> In my box I have a flea,
> Renee, she's hopping happily.
> The bell is ringing now for tea,
> My flea,
> I know she'll wait for me.

I started to put the notebook back in my desk, but then changed my mind and put it with my schoolbooks. I'd keep it in my desk at school. That way, I couldn't forget a poem before I had a chance to write it down.

It was cold in the house, so I went and got a sweat-shirt out of my closet. The closet was so jammed with junk that I had to hold all the stuff in with one hand, while I closed the door with the other. I should have written a poem about a closet full of junk. A closet poem. I once heard somebody say that someone was a closet poet, like he didn't want anyone to know he was a poet. Just like me. A closet poet with a closet poem. Pop would laugh at that if I could tell him. He loves puns. But I couldn't tell him because he doesn't know anything at all about my poetry. He wouldn't laugh at my poems, I know that, but I feel a little shy about them.

I went back to the kitchen and began looking in the refrigerator. Eggs. Cheese. Peanut butter. Why was the peanut butter in the refrigerator? Two tomatoes wrapped in plastic. Some margarine. A can of chocolate syrup. That was it. I was sick of cheese omelettes and Egg Pizza, and I didn't feel like going to the store.

"Hey, Pop," I said. "How do you think eggs would taste with peanut butter in them? You know, like we put cheese in the middle, only put in the peanut butter?"

He scratched his neck. "Probably awful. But we don't know till we try it, right?" He gave me that funny smile that just sort of spreads and spreads.

"Right," I said, and I smiled back.

"Go to it."

"You gotta eat it, though," I said.

"You know I will."

He would, too. We have this deal—if one guy makes supper, the other one eats it, no matter what. And Pop never breaks a promise.

So I made it—scrambled eggs with peanut butter, and some toast with margarine, and coffee for Pop and for me, too, since we were out of milk.

With the first bite, I almost threw up. "Bleech!" I put down my fork.

Pop shrugged. "Not terrific." But he went right on eating.

"Not terrific? It's vomitrocious."

"Oh, it's not *that* bad." He kept right on eating it, stopping now and then to wash the whole mess down with gulps of coffee.

"Pop," I said. "You don't have to eat this."

"Hey," he said. "A deal's a deal. Besides, it's not really all that bad."

I swallowed hard and picked up my fork. I guessed if he could do it, I could, too. Fortunately, the peanut butter stayed pretty much in a blob in the center of the eggs. So I ate around that part of it, and when I was almost finished, and all that was left was the peanut butter part, I swallowed the whole thing without biting it or tasting it all that much. Down it went, and I washed it all away with coffee.

Pop was watching me, and as I swallowed and made a face, he said, "Yuck," for me.

When I put down my coffee cup, Pop reached for my hand and laid his over mine on the table. "Now," he said. "Tell me the truth. What really happened today?"

"Hey, nothing. I told you, nothing." How could I tell him? How could I tell him that I couldn't bear to move again, that I was finally happy? That I had a friend? That everybody in the class knew me—"Kevin Corbett eats flies—spiders, too!" Maybe even goldfish. Although I didn't want to think about the goldfish part right then.

Pop nodded, but it seemed to me that a shadow came across his face, that same kind of lost look that he had six years ago when Mom died. It was a look that never went away until he and I started traveling around together. Pop always said it was for more money that we moved, so he could get a better job, though I never noticed that his jobs were any better, and we sure didn't seem to have more money. Not that we were poor or anything, but we didn't seem to have more money in the new place than in the old. So I knew that it was something else that made him move, but I suspected that he didn't know any more than I did what it was.

But seeing that sad look on his face, I had to say something quickly. "Okay," I said. "Something happened."

Pop nodded, and waited for me to go on.

"Well, there's this new kid. Bailey her name is. . . ."

He nodded encouragement. He's the best listener I know.

"Well, see . . ." I paused. I hate lying to Pop! Yeah, Bailey was a problem, and the goldfish thing was weird. But I'd take care of it. It was the thought of moving again. But how could I say that to Pop when he needs to move to be happy? I *had* to lie. "Well," I said, "I've gotten to be kind of the leader in that class. You know, everybody knows me and stuff. And in walks Bailey—the skinniest, littlest and the messiest kid in the world—and she sort of—I don't know, takes over?"

Pop was nodding and smiling again. "I think I got the picture," he said. "No room at the top for two."

"Right," I said.

"I'll bet you'll show her, though. You'll show her pretty soon who's who."

"Yeah," I said. "I guess. But she's pretty tough."

"So are you, son." Pop stood up and put his hand for a moment on my head. "So are you."

Something about the way he said it—he seemed to mean it in a different way, like not really *tough*, but . . . strong, maybe? When I looked up at him, he seemed so serious.

I tried to smile at him, then looked away. How could he think I was tough—strong? I wasn't strong. We were going to move again, and I felt just plain sick.

And tomorrow I had to face Bailey, and maybe chew up a goldfish. There was only one thing to look forward to. Maybe we'd move before Goldie died. But I'd rather chew up a goldfish, I'd rather chew up a whole fleet of goldfish, rather than move away. And there was no way I could tell Pop that. There was no way at all.

3

NEXT MORNING I was awake super-early. I could hear Pop moving around getting ready for work, making coffee and my sandwiches for lunch in the kitchen. Pop always gets up really early because the crew he paints with gets started as soon as it gets light. Even though I was awake, I wasn't tempted to get up and talk to him. I had to think. I had two big problems now—moving, and a half-dead gold-fish. The moving part I couldn't do anything about, not just yet anyway, and probably not later, either. Anyway, Pop had said he'd wait a month or so. Today's problem was Goldie. I had to figure out a way to keep him alive. Nobody, not even Bailey, would expect me to chew up a live goldfish. So, I would have to do some research—fast—on how to keep a goldfish in good health.

As soon as I heard Pop leave for work, I got up, dressed, and got started. We don't have many books, but we do have this fantastic set of encyclopedias. Pop bought them last year when we'd been traveling for two months. He thought it would help educate me if I read them while we traveled.

Many of our things we hadn't bothered to unpack, and they were still in boxes against the kitchen wall. But the encyclopedias we had put in a bookcase in the dining room. I took out the ''F'' book for fish, and the ''G'' book for goldfish. The only thing I could learn was that fish needed air as well as water, and also how an air pump works, by bubbling up water into the air to get oxygen, and then settling down again.

Okay, if air was what Goldie needed, air was what he'd get. I didn't have an air pump, but I did have a plastic straw. I took it out and put it with my schoolbooks. Then, even though it was only seven o'clock, I gulped down my breakfast and ran for school. If Goldie had made it through the night, I'd make sure he made it through the day.

I'm coming, Goldie, I'm coming, I told him in my mind.

I raced up the school steps, and yanked at the door. Locked.

Shoot! Mr. Luparello, the janitor, wasn't there yet. I looked around the parking lot. No cars. Nobody was there yet.

Hurry, hurry, hurry, I prayed.

I looked at my watch. I'd already been there ten minutes. Maybe I should meditate. I'd heard people talk about it on TV. You sort of think things, like send good thoughts to yourself or to someone else. Why not to a fish? So I sat for a minute with my eyes closed, sending good thoughts to Goldie. *Don't die. I'm coming with air.*

I opened my eyes when I heard a car door slam. Mr. Luparello. He came tottering up the walk, his head bent, a brown paper bag clutched in one hand, his keys dangling in the other. The keys were clanking away because his hand was shaking so much.

I could tell he hadn't seen me sitting there, so I spoke

softly, not wanting to startle him. I was afraid he'd have a heart attack right there and I'd never get in the school.

" 'Morning, Mr. Luparello," I said in my most polite voice. I wanted to be sure he'd let me in.

He stepped back two whole steps like he thought I was going to attack him.

"Yes?" he wheezed at me.

"I need to come in," I said.

"Awful early." He squinted at me suspiciously.

Hurry!

I smiled, and tried not to look too impatient. "I have a special project," I said. That wasn't a lie.

He came up to the door and began stabbing his keys at the lock. His hand was shaking so much that he missed the first two tries. The third time, he got the key in, but it must have been the wrong one because the lock wouldn't turn. He took the key out and tried a different one.

"Can I help?" I said.

Wrong thing to say. He took the key out and looked at me. "Been doin' this for thirty-seven years," he said. He didn't move to unlock the door.

"Oh." I tried to smile.

He went back to working the locks, and after about another thirty-seven years, he finally had the door opened. He went in first, then held the door for me, but only about three inches wide, as if he had to hold back a whole horde of people.

"Thanks," I said as I pushed past him and headed for the stairs.

As I took the steps two at a time, I heard him say something, but I couldn't tell what it was.

Hold on, Goldie, hold on. Help is on the way.

The classroom door was open, and I turned on the lights and hurried over to the fish tank. "Hey, Goldie, how's it going?"

Not real well. Not at all. Goldie was at the top of the water, floating on his back, belly up.

I scooped him out and looked at him close, just to be sure. Dead. For a minute, holding him in my hand, I thought about what it would be like to chew him up. The thought was so disgusting that I quickly dropped him back into the fish tank.

For this I raced to school! If Mr. Luparello only knew that this was why . . . Mr. Luparello! The answer to my problem! Janitors always threw away things. That was their job. I'd just throw away the dead fish, and tell anyone who asked that I saw Mr. Luparello doing it.

I rolled up my sleeve, because by now Goldie was halfway down in the water, sort of stuck to the side of the bowl. For the second time, I scooped Goldie out.

Voices in the hall . . . Miss Holt, and . . . *Bailey?*

I stuck the goldfish in my pocket and started toward the door. They wouldn't know he was in my pocket. I'd take him to the lavatory and flush.

But no, what if they asked, if they looked in the bowl right away? And they would, too—Bailey would. Would I be able to lie right off like that, say Mr. Luparello had done it? And how would I know that he had? What if they asked him?

The voices were closer, and I could hear Miss Holt's heels clicking on the corridor floor.

I took Goldie out of my pocket. Bits of lint and fuzz

were stuck to him. I dropped him back in the bowl just as Miss Holt and Bailey came into the room.

"Well, Kevin, you're early!" Miss Holt's voice was surprised, but not as suspicious as Mr. Luparello's had been. Her eyebrows went up so far under her bangs that they disappeared. She's really awfully pretty for a teacher. In fact, every girl in the class tries to imitate the way she does her hair, especially those big, long bangs. Everybody but Bailey. Miss Holt smiled at me.

"Yes. Well, I just wondered how Goldie was."

Mistake. Now they would know right away that he was dead, and I wouldn't have another chance to ditch him.

"How is he?" Bailey asked, but she surprised me by not looking in the tank to see. She just grinned at me.

She had probably murdered him during the night.

I made a face at her.

"Oooh, poor little thing!" Miss Holt said. She bent over the fish tank and peered in, cooing like it was a real live baby in there. "I don't have very good luck with fish," she said. She shook her head, then straightened up and turned to me. "Kevin, would you get rid of him for me? Just take him in the lavatory and . . ."

"Oh, no!" Bailey had a hand on Miss Holt's arm. "Oh, no, Miss Holt! Please don't do that. Just leave him here for today, and I'll take him home and bury him. See, I have a whole lot of pets buried in my yard. I want to bury him with the others."

Bailey had this super-sincere look on her face, and if I hadn't been so anxious to get rid of the fish, I'd have given her credit for that look. It was one that any teacher would fall for. She was a real pro.

"It'll stink by this afternoon," I said. Again I rolled up my sleeve and started to stick my arm in the tank, but Miss Holt stopped me.

"Well, Kevin, I don't think it will . . . smell . . . that fast. And if it's important to Bailey . . ."

"Oh, it *is*, Miss Holt," Bailey said.

I glared at her, but Miss Holt was nodding as if she totally understood. If she only knew.

"All right then," she said. She turned to me. "We'll just leave it there for now."

"It'll stink," I said, one more time. I knew I had lost, but you could never tell, so I said it anyway. And then I went back to my desk and sat down.

All right, Bailey, I thought. *You might have won this one. But just you wait.*

All the pets buried in her yard! She had just moved here—unless she had dug up all her pets and moved them with her. Maybe I should say that to Holt? How could she fall for that line?

But I knew I couldn't make too much of a scene in front of Bailey, or she'd accuse me of being chicken. I'd have to wait and see if she'd leave the room for a second. Then I could tell Holt quietly.

But of course, Bailey just sat herself down at her desk, head bent over a notebook, doing her Best-Little-Girl-in-the-World routine. I wanted to smack her.

I sat there, my heart hammering like crazy, globs of saliva swimming around in my mouth. Was I going to throw up? When I chewed the thing, *would* I throw up—right in front of the whole class?

I had one last urge to sneak up to the front and somehow ditch the fish, but kids were coming into the classroom by then. One by one, they were stopping in front of the fish tank to look in. And then one by one, they'd turn and look first at me, and then at Bailey. But nobody said a word except Brant.

"Oh, hey!" he said, really loud. "Goldie's dead. Miss Holt, do you want me to get rid of him for you?" He went and stood by her desk, leaning on it with one elbow, and looking up into her face. He's the biggest flirt I know. He's always telling Miss Holt that he's in love with her, and she always says, "Oh, Brant!" But you can tell that she doesn't mind.

"No, thanks, Brant," she said. "Bailey has other plans for him."

You could hear everyone in the class suck in their breath at the same time, and about four people said, "What!" all at once.

Miss Holt looked puzzled, but she said quietly, "Bailey wants to bury him properly, that's all."

She frowned when a couple of people started to laugh.

Brant just shrugged. He headed back to his desk, but he stopped at mine first. "I tried," he said.

"I know. Thanks." Then I added, "Some burial. In my stomach."

He shrugged. "Five bucks is five bucks." He went and sat down.

The rest of the morning went by in a blur. My brain kept saying it was no big deal, just a couple of bites. And my stomach kept saying, "Throw up, throw up," even though I hadn't eaten the stupid thing yet. I watched the big clock on the wall, and prayed that somebody would unplug it or something and it would never get to ten-thirty.

24

Most days it just drags, but this day it was as if someone had wound it up in super-fast motion.

Then it was ten-thirty, and Miss Holt left the room with her thermos. She left the door open, and put Janie in charge again.

I didn't wait for Bailey to start. Right away I stood up and went to the front of the room. I peeked out into the hall. Only Holt's back was visible in the door across the hall.

"Okay, Bailey," I said softly. "Where's your five bucks?"

She came up and stood beside me, really close, and stuck a crumpled-up bill in my hand. Then she said, very quietly, so no one could hear but me, "You don't have to do it. I'll give you a way out if you want."

For just a second, I looked at her, tempted. But I turned away and said, "Here goes."

I stuck my hand in the fish tank and scooped Goldie out.

Brant came up and handed me a piece of paper to wrap it in. It was only a tiny scrap—I guess so I wouldn't have to swallow too much paper—and my hands were shaking so that when I wrapped it around the fish, Goldie slid out and fell on the floor.

Brant immediately picked it up, dipped it in the fish tank to wash it off, and handed it back to me.

This time I wrapped it without dropping it, although my hands were still shaking.

The only sound in the room was silence, and the roar that my heart was making in my ears.

I started to say, "Here goes," again, but my tongue

was stuck to the roof of my mouth. I just opened my mouth and stuck in the fish, paper and all, way in the back between my back teeth.

And bit it.

It crunched. Like jelly beans with bones in them.

I instantly felt sick, not just in my stomach, but all over.

Don't think. Don't think.

Another bite.

It's only hard jellied candy. Not a pet goldfish.

Bit again. And it began to come apart in my mouth, a piece of it sliding across my tongue.

I gulped and swallowed. It went partway down, and then my throat closed around it, squeezed it, and it started to come back up again.

I made myself swallow hard, gulping again, forcing it down. I felt it slide across my throat, a slimy, jellied mess.

The paper stayed in my mouth, and I spit it out. Then, really casually, I turned to Janie.

"I'm going to the lavatory," I said.

Brant was still beside me. "Me, too!" he said. He whispered to me, "You sick?"

I nodded.

Out in the hall, Miss Holt turned and looked at us, but we didn't say anything. We walked as fast as we could, not running, just fast-walking. But as we did, I heard someone in class say, "Hey, Bailey? Does it still count if he throws it up?"

I wanted to wait and hear what she answered, but the need to get to the bathroom was stronger. I didn't know if I'd make it in time.

4

I DIDN'T THROW IT UP, although for the rest of the day I wished I had. My stomach rumbled, and I kept getting globs of saliva in my mouth. I sat in the bathroom half the afternoon, and was there so long after school that even Brant didn't wait for me.

I went outside and down the school steps, and it seemed weird to have nobody around, no kids yelling and all. Then, just as I got around the corner of the school I saw this person in front of the paper stand halfway down the block. Bailey. Even though I couldn't see her face, I could tell who it was. Nobody else could be that big-deal-self-important looking. She stood by the paper stand like she was a Porsche with a perfect right to be parked there.

Some Porsche, I thought. She needs to go through a car wash.

When I got closer to her, she started sliding out toward me, like her car was heading into traffic.

I pretended like I had just thought of something very important I had to do, and I had to run home to do it. I started running, weaving in and out of people on the sidewalk.

She began running, too, right alongside me.

"Want to race?" she asked, after about half a block.

"No."

"Then why are you running?"

"I just thought of something."

"What?"

I stopped suddenly, and she stopped, too. "Ever think that it might not be any of your business?" I asked.

"Why not?"

Biggest pain I'd ever met! *Why not*? How did you answer a question like that?

"Because," I said. Even before she said anything, I thought, *What a stupid answer*.

"That's a stupid answer," she said.

I glared at her.

As if she hadn't noticed, she asked, "You throw up?"

"No! I didn't 'throw up!' "

"Wish you did?"

I didn't answer right away. "Maybe," I said.

"Did it taste gross?"

"I didn't taste it."

"You really did chew it, didn't you?"

"Yeah."

"I didn't make you prove it." She shuddered. "I could tell."

She didn't say anything more, just walked along next to me. After a while she asked, "Ever see a green mouse?"

"*Green*? No."

"I have."

"Big deal."

"I have one. It's mine."

"So?"

She just shrugged.

We walked a while more silently, and then I couldn't help my curiosity. "So, how did it get green?"

"Don't know. Some guys chopped down a tree, and in the base of it there was this nest with a mother mouse and some babies. One of the babies was green."

"*Really* green? Bright green?"

"Greenish. Kind of."

I wondered why she was telling me all this, or why she had waited for me in the first place.

"You keep them all or just the *green* one?" I asked. I meant it to come out sarcastic-sounding, but it came out as a real question.

"I kept them all. Took them to the vet. He said the color could be some deficiency or maybe something it ate. But it's still green."

"You spent *money* taking mice to the vet?"

She pulled a strand of her skinny hair across her mouth and chewed on it. "I know how to make money. I keep thinking up lots of new ways."

I gave her one of my "Sure you do," looks, but I couldn't help wondering if she really did. She had given me my five dollars, and not only that, she'd had it with her when she made the bet—didn't even have to go home for it.

"So?" she said. "Wanna see it? I could bring it over to your house."

My house? Why not hers? But I didn't want to see any stupid green mouse of hers anyway, not at my house, not at hers.

"No," I said.

"Why not?"

"Because!" I answered, and even though she had made fun of that answer before, still I said it. But this time I glared at her.

She shrugged and looked away. "It nibbles on you," she said. But it was halfhearted the way she said it, like she wasn't really expecting to persuade me.

We walked on, and I saw how she'd stuck her hands down in the pockets of her jeans, deep down, and how she hunched up her shoulders when she did it. It made her look even littler and skinnier than she was. There were two pointy knobs on each shoulder.

"So, where'd you move here from?" I asked. Not that I really wanted to know. But she didn't have to look so pitiful.

"Oh, here and there," she answered. She waved a hand sort of aimlessly, but she smiled. "They move me around a lot."

"Who?" I asked.

"Them." She looked at me and for the first time I noticed how big her eyes were—wide and very green. They were so big they seemed to take over her face. Maybe her face wasn't really that little and skinny. Maybe it just seemed that way because her eyes took up so much of it.

"It wouldn't take long to get the mouse," she said. "I could come on my bike."

"Sure," I said. "Why not? Do you know where I live?"

"Yeah. I know. See you." And she turned and took off running back in the direction of the school.

I watched her run, her legs pumping, her hair flying out behind her. That girl could run!

Then I turned and went toward home again, wondering what was the matter with me—letting a skinny girl persuade me to see a green mouse. She had probably painted it green just to show off.

I had just let myself in with my key and made myself a peanut butter and banana sandwich when I looked out the window and saw her coming down the street. She was riding an old, old, *old* bike, the kind with wide, fat wheels. It was meant for somebody twice her size, and she had to stand up to pump it. She was trying to steer it with one hand, and was sort of wiggling back and forth across the street. With the other hand she was holding onto her chest, as though she was holding the creepy little mouse inside her jacket. She knew where she was going, though, and she headed straight into the yard.

I took my sandwich and went out on the porch.

She got off her bike and let it fall against a tree, then came up the steps to the porch. She looked at the house. "Where's your mom?"

"Don't have one," I said. I looked straight at her when I said that. It's something I had practiced right after Mom died—being sort of matter-of-fact, so no one would feel sorry for me. I still did it now, even though I didn't have to anymore because it didn't matter so much.

Bailey nodded. "Me, neither," she said. "Brothers? Sisters?"

"Nope."

Again she nodded. "Me, neither."

"Just me and Pop," I said. "He's cool."

"Yeah?" She sat down then and reached inside her jacket. Then, very carefully, she scooped out this little blackish-gray mouse. It wasn't green at all. She made a circle with her hands so that she looked like she belonged in that ad on TV: "You're in good hands with Allstate"—

and the mouse scurried around inside the circle of her hands. Then he pooped right on her palm, but she didn't seem to mind.

She let him go free of her hands then, and he scrambled up to her shoulder.

"He doesn't look green to me," I said.

She felt for him on her neck, then brought him down gently. She turned him over, belly up, and parted his fur. "Look here," she said.

I looked where she had parted the fur and I had to admit that he looked a little greenish. Actually, I would have said yellow. But maybe all mice had yellowish skin if you looked hard enough.

She turned him upright again, and then let him loose so that he ran back up her arm to her neck. She smiled, and for a second I thought, *She's pretty!* But I shook my head. Weird. I was getting weird.

"So, how'd you know where I live?" I asked.

"I know lots of things. When you move to a new place, you gotta learn everything about everybody in a hurry."

"So, how do you learn?"

"I have ways." She looked me over as if she was measuring me. "I know more about you than you'd ever guess."

I was going to say, "Yeah, like what?" but I didn't. I suddenly got the feeling that maybe she knew things I didn't want her to. Like about my poems. So instead I said, "How can you let that thing poop all over you? You stink."

She shrugged. "It washes off."

I moved a few inches away from her.

"So are you going to move again?" she asked.

"W, t?"

"You move almost as much as I do. How come? At least I have a reason."

"Yeah?" I didn't see any sense in giving her any more information than she already had. So I made my voice mean, and my eyes into little slits. "So what's your reason?"

"I'm in foster homes. They put me with stupid people, so when I get sick of them I do something so they'll kick me out."

I'll bet you do. But I didn't say it out loud. Instead I said, "You *like* moving?"

"Yeah." She brought the mouse down from her shoulder very carefully and cupped it in her hands. She stroked the mouse with one finger. Her fingers were amazingly long and thin. Her voice went so soft that for a moment I thought she was talking to the mouse. "New places are nice, aren't they?" she said. "Lots of new things to see. I lived in New Mexico once. Pigs and goats ran around in the yard. I liked that."

She was quiet.

"I lived in Arizona once," I said. "People had horses."

"Yeah?" She looked at me with her great big eyes again, and again I thought that weird thing: *Pretty*!

I looked away.

Bailey patted the mouse again. "Animals are cool," she said. "They don't care if they've never seen you before. If you're nice to them, they're nice back."

She took up and put the mouse close to her face for a moment. "Gotta go. Gotta take care of Matt."

"Who's he?"

"Her kid. But he's okay." Then she added, "See you tomorrow?"

"We're in the same class, aren't we?" I said. I didn't want her making any assumptions, like that we'd be friends or anything.

" 'Course," she said. And she put the mouse back in her jacket, got on her bike and rode off.

5

I SPENT the rest of that week dodging Bailey. Didn't she know that boys hung around with boys and girls hung around with girls? Man, was she dumb. She acted like she came from another planet instead of another state. I asked Brant one day if he knew what state she'd moved from, and he said, "The state of confusion." And then almost fell over his own feet, laughing. It was a really dumb answer, but his laugh is so funny that I couldn't help laughing with him. But what Bailey was doing wasn't funny at all.

She kept showing up on the field where we played Capture the Flag, and since she was there, we had to choose her when we chose up sides, although she was always chosen last. Once the game started, she wasn't dumb enough to actually stick to me, but I could always feel her eyes on me. Once in a while, like if we were on base together, I thought I heard her say, "Kevin?" really quietly, but I always managed to be looking the other way.

For Pete's sake, couldn't she find another friend? Why did she have to choose *me*? I didn't want to be her friend. Although every so often, that look in her eyes, or the sometimes soft way she spoke, made me think that maybe she'd be nice to get to know.

Fortunately that kind of thought didn't last long.

The worst of it was the way she waited around for me, both before and after school. After school, Brant and I had a system figured out. We just ignored her like she wasn't there, and after a while, even though she kept on walking with us, she gave up trying to talk to us. But that was going home from school. Going to school was harder. I walked alone, because Brant got a ride every day from his mom on her way to work. Bailey had a way of lying in wait for me, never in the same place twice.

Then one morning, about a week after she showed me her great green mouse, I was walking alone to school and she appeared. She sprang up from behind the news-stand like she was one of those pop-up dolls in a pop-up book. Now what?

"What are you doing here?" I asked.

"Waiting for you, whatta you think?"

I started fast-walking.

She fast-walked, too.

"What for?" I asked.

"Why not?" she said.

"Look," I said. "Find some other friends. Some girls."

She screwed up her face. "Those girls are so boring they're practically dead. And those are the nice ones." She continued to ugly up her face, then added, "The others are plain sickening.

"Miss Holt?" she said, and she made her voice super-high, in imitation of Janie, and she hung onto the sides of her jeans' legs as though they were a skirt. "Oh, Miss

Ho . . . olt?" She blinked super-fast. "Look at my blinking, blinking eyes, and my pretty, pretty handwriting. I am smart. I am sweet. I am teacher's pet." She brought her voice back to normal. "And I am going to throw up."

I couldn't help laughing. She did sound like Janie and some of her friends. "Yeah," I said. "But there must be somebody who's okay."

"Name one."

I thought. There were a couple of girls who were okay. Stephanie. Violet. Jennifer. But then I looked at Bailey and I saw what she meant. Violet was nice, but somehow I couldn't picture her hanging out with Bailey. Violet was just too . . . too *clean*, or something. Bailey would probably call it something else.

Stephanie? Stephanie's nice, but maybe too nice. Nice did not work with Bailey.

Jennifer? I shook my head. Too bossy. She and Bailey would have wars.

Bailey was watching me, and she nodded as if she'd been following my thoughts the whole way.

After a while, she reached into her pocket and took out a little plastic bag. She handed it to me. "Here, these are for you."

I held it up and looked at it. Bunches of dead flies—fat blue ones and smaller ones like babies, some of them so dried up the wings had broken off.

"A new supply," she said. "The whole last batch that I snapped off the windowsill I saved for you."

"Thanks," I said.

She nodded.

"Listen," I said, all of a sudden and in a rush because I was afraid that if I didn't say it fast, I'd change my mind. "Why don't we meet again tomorrow morning? We could talk some more."

Maybe I was getting crazy, but I did kind of like being with her.

"Sure," she said.

We were getting close to school, and I didn't want to be seen walking in with her, so I slowed down. "Okay, tomorrow?" I said.

"Tomorrow." She slowed, too.

I stopped dead.

She stopped, too.

Geez! Couldn't she even take a hint?

"I said tomorrow!" I said again.

"I heard you."

"Well, what are you waiting for then?"

She squinted at me for a long time. "If you want to get rid of me, why don't you have the guts to say so?"

"I'm saying so." But I had to squeeze the words past this funny feeling that suddenly came up in my throat.

She turned around and went on alone, her hands stuffed down into her pockets in the funny way she has that makes her shoulders hunch up and the pointy bones stick out like little wings.

"Sticks to me like bubble gum," I muttered.

But the lump wouldn't go away from my throat.

Hell.

"Wait up!" I called.

She acted like she hadn't heard me.

"Hey!"

She didn't turn around.

I ran until I caught up with her. "Why didn't you wait?"

She walked even faster, not answering me or looking at me or anything.

"Look," I said. "Do you want a friend or not?"

I was so surprised when the words came out, that I almost put a hand over my mouth. Had I really said that? I hadn't meant to. It was only that I was thinking that she didn't have any friends. I think that's what I meant.

She took a deep breath and stuck her hands even deeper into her pockets and she muttered something. I thought she said, "Maybe, maybe not." But I couldn't tell for sure.

And then she took off, running like crazy toward the school.

Maybe, maybe not. What kind of a stupid answer was that? For the whole morning, I kept looking at her, trying to get her attention, but she acted like I wasn't even in the classroom. I even thought of swallowing some flies for her—I could even tell everybody that she'd given them to me. But then I thought I'd better not. It wasn't till we were on our way back in from recess that she spoke to me at all.

I had expected her to come to the boys' playground like she always did, but she didn't show up. I didn't see her on the girls' playground, either, even though I kept looking for her. It was only on our way back into school that I looked over my shoulder and saw her on the steps behind me in the girls' line. She was right in front of Janie and Violet.

Right away, I dropped the football I was carrying and

ran down the steps to retrieve it, pretending I had dropped it by accident. I waited until the girls' line caught up.

When Bailey was alongside me, I started up the steps next to her. "Where were you?" I asked very quietly, trying to talk without moving my lips so no one would know I was talking to her.

"What do you care, Slug-Slime?" She said it really loudly.

Violet and Janie put their hands over their mouths and made those squeaking sounds that only girls make, like they had hamsters hidden in their cheeks.

"Listen!" I was getting mad, and it was harder to talk without moving my lips. "You just don't understand the rules in this school. We can be friends outside school. Maybe. But—"

"Forget it, Pig-Snout."

"Have it your way." I looked her up and down, from her floppy brown hair, to her sweater two sizes too big for her, all the way down to her feet in the smallest sneakers I've ever seen on a fifth-grader. I was looking for just the right name to call her, but the only one that came to me was the one I call Violet—"Barrel-Butt.'" But Bailey was so skinny she didn't have any butt at all. So right away, I had the idea.

"Mosquito-Ass," I said. And I took the steps two at a time till I caught up with Brant.

6

AT SUPPER that night, I decided I needed to talk to Pop. It was his turn to cook—Camp Stew and baloney sandwiches—and I waited till we were almost finished before I started. "I've been thinking about . . . somebody," I said. "I don't know what to do."

"Yeah?" Right away Pop put down his fork and was all attention, the way he always is when I talk to him.

"Sounds really strange," I said. "You have to promise not to laugh."

"I won't laugh."

"It's that girl . . . you know . . . the new one?"

"Bailey?"

"Yeah." I scraped at the varnish on the tabletop with my fingernail. "Did you ever have a girl for a friend? I don't mean a *girl*friend. I mean a friend?"

"Sure," Pop said. "They're the nicest kind."

I looked up quick, but he wasn't laughing at me. His head was tilted a little, as if he was remembering.

"But I'm not sure if I really like her."

Pop waited.

"See," I said. "She's kinda weird. But she's funny, too. And man, if she wants something, does she stick! She's followed me around for a whole week. You know that?"

Pop nodded like he knew.

"But I don't know if I like her or not," I said again. "Half of me likes her, and half of me feels sorry for her. But mostly I think I like her." I peeled the varnish off my fingernail. "If only she wasn't a girl."

"Yeah." Pop scratched his neck. "You sure you can't be friends anyway?"

I picked up my fork and started eating again. "I don't know," I said.

But Pop didn't pick up his fork. "I'd do it. Who cares what the guys say? It *is* them you're worrying about, right?"

I nodded.

"Go for it," Pop said. "There aren't enough friends in this world that we can waste one who comes looking."

I couldn't help laughing. "She's not exactly looking. Just sort of hanging around."

"She's got good taste," Pop said. "He—heck . . . go for it."

He grinned at me. We've both been trying to stop swearing ever since the beginning of the school year when Miss Holt gave me . . . heck . . . for it.

"So do it," Pop said. "You got time left. We're not going anywhere for a while yet."

Going. Why was he always bringing that up? I didn't answer.

"But," he said. "I do have some . . . news for you."

It was about the move. I could tell instantly by the hesitant way he said it.

"Yeah?" *Don't look up. Don't.*

"Yeah, well see . . ." Pop stood up suddenly. He swung his chair around backwards and sat down again, straddling it like it was a horse. He looked at me once over the back of it, then away. With one finger, he began tracing the swirled pattern of the carving in the back of the chair. He watched his finger closely, as if he didn't want to miss even one tiny swirl.

"See, I've been meaning to tell you," he said. "I think I've found a new car, see? Not brand-new, you know how I feel about that. But a nice, fixed-up older one. The guy's going to put on new tires. What do you think of that?" He smiled at me. "Just like that, the dealer offered it. 'Four new tires go with it,' he said. So I said, 'You got a deal.' And he's going to tune it up and balance the wheels, and it'll be ready to go as soon as I get the money. Maybe in a coupla' weeks."

I couldn't even look at him.

Weeks. After we got the new car we'd be moving.

There was a pause, and I knew he was waiting. Waiting for me to say, "Great! Let's go!" Just like I always did for him. I even opened my mouth to say it, but the words just stayed inside.

So Pop went on, but more slowly, sounding even timid. "I thought we'd just clean up in here and pack up and then be off? You know us, son. It doesn't take much for us to pack, does it?"

I looked up and he was smiling at me, but it wasn't that clear, bright smile like before when we were talking about Bailey. His eyebrows were up, and I knew he was still waiting.

So I gave him what I knew he waited for. "Sure, Pop," I said. "Sounds good."

There was silence then. Just the electric stove made little tick-tick sounds under the pot with the remains of the stew.

I'm not a great liar, and Pop knows me too well, and the silence went on for a long time. But there *was* something I was interested in, so I'd distract him with that. "What kind of car?" I asked. "What color?"

"You're going to love it." Pop stood up and began carrying dishes to the sink. "It's a Chevy. Red. Well, sort of maroon."

I stood up too, and took the dishes from his hands. "I'm the dish-doer," I said. "You made supper."

"I'll give you the night off." Pop grinned at me.

"No way. A deal's a deal."

"Okay, then," Pop said. "Tell you what. While you do the dishes, I'll begin packing up some stuff here—or at least going through some of this stuff."

He began rummaging through some of the cardboard boxes that had been stacked against the far wall of the kitchen since we moved in last April, spilling out junk.

Should I say it to him? Should I say. . . . *Let's not go, Pop. This is a good place. I like it here. I have friends . . . Brant, maybe even . . . well, maybe she's not a friend, but Bailey's okay. . . . And even Miss Holt isn't a bad teacher. And I'm the big deal in that class. I don't want to move anymore. It was all right when I was a little kid, but I don't want to do it anymore. I don't want to have to start over every six months or so. Couldn't we stay?*

44

But the words stayed right inside my head.

"Remember when you used to make maps?" Pop interrupted my thinking. He was holding up an old notebook of mine that he had dug out of the box. "Everywhere we went, you used to make a map. The state, our neighborhood, our own street. You even made a map of your school once, right down to each single classroom. Remember?"

He flipped through the notebook, smiling. "Remember?" He looked up at me.

"Yeah, I remember."

I did. We moved so much I used to think I'd get lost all the time, so I made maps. I'd never told Pop why.

"You were a funny little kid," he said softly, and he was still smiling as he bent over the box again, sorting through the stuff.

Watching him, I thought: he looks happy. He always looks happy when we're getting ready to move.

That night for the first time in a long time, I took Bahr to bed with me. I always used to sleep with Bahr, but lately, I only take him to bed when I'm feeling lonely or something. He's sort of a medium-sized bear, with the softest fur, and with a stomach that squeezes in. But it's his eyes that are special. When you look right into his face, his eyes look back at you like he's real, and like he understands exactly what you're thinking.

I had just gotten into bed when Pop opened the door to say good night. I quickly stuffed Bahr down under the covers.

" 'Night son," Pop said quietly.

" 'Night, Pop." He stood by the door for a minute, then came over to the bed.

I stuffed Bahr further down so I was lying on him.

Pop tucked in the covers on one side, then went around to the other side of the bed to tuck them in there. Then he went to the window and did something with the shade. When he was finished, he didn't leave.

I got the feeling that he was working up his courage to say something, but whatever it was, I didn't want him to say it.

So I said, " 'Night," once again, and I made my voice super-sleepy.

" 'Night, son." But he still stood there.

He was going to say that he was sorry we were moving, that he hoped I didn't mind much. Something like that. I couldn't have him say that. Not anything.

I made my breathing so heavy and so regular that I was practically snoring.

"Son?"

I breathed deeper, and sighed, and I didn't answer. But I kept my eyes open a tiny bit and I watched him.

He came to the bed and stood beside me.

He put his hand against my cheek so softly that if I hadn't been watching him I'd have thought it was only a shadow that touched me.

Then he tiptoed from my room and closed the door behind me.

I pulled Bahr out from under the covers, fluffed up his fur, and then put my head on him like he was a pillow, just the way I used to do when I was really small.

NEXT MORNING I left for school early, partly because it felt sad in the house, just looking at that box Pop had already begun to pack up, and partly because I kind of wanted to see Bailey. I looked for her in all the places she'd been hiding for the past week before she'd pop out at me, but I couldn't find her anywhere.

So, what'd I care? But I looked anyway.

I checked by the newsstand, and then by the path through the empty lot, and by the alley next to the candy store. No Bailey, anywhere. Finally, I had to give up and I went on to school alone. There she was, sitting on the corner of the school steps. She had her elbows jammed into her knees, and her jaw planted on her fists. And the meanest look on her face that I've seen anywhere since I saw those movies about the man-eating sharks.

I walked right up to her. "So, you want to be friends or not?" I asked.

She squinted up her eyes at me. "In school or out?"

"Out," I said.

"No."

Staring contest. Man, did she look mean. But she spoke first. "Both or nothing."

"You don't understand!" I said.

"I understand, *Mr*. Kevin Corbett." Super-sarcastic. "You're chicken."

"Nobody calls me chicken."

"Chicken."

I'd been standing and she'd been sitting, but she stood up then, face to face with me. More chin to face, since she was such a shrimp.

I made a fist. I swear, if she'd been a guy I'd have popped her.

Her huge green eyes didn't even blink.

Oh, hell.

I stuffed my fist in my pocket and sat down, my back to her. I don't know when she left, but when I turned around a while later, she was gone.

In class that morning, after all the morning exercises were done, Miss Holt announced that we were going to be writing letters. "Friendly letters," she called them. We were supposed to write to our grandparents. "Something special," Miss Holt said. "Telling them how special they are to you." That's because the second grade was having something called "Grandparents' Day," and the whole school was supposed to participate in some way. Our way was going to be by writing letters. Holt went on to say that although some people's grandparents might be dead, we could choose a favorite aunt or uncle.

Right away, about a hundred hands went up.

"Which aunt or uncle?"

"Any one you want, Stephanie."

"Which grandparent if they're all alive?"

"So, you want to be friends or not?"

"Any grandparent, Owen."

"Do we have to use complete sentences?"

"We always use complete sentences, Jennifer."

"Could I write to you instead, Miss Holt?"

"*No*, Brant!"

By the time the questions were all asked, I had already half-finished my letter. I have only one grandparent anyway, my Grandpa out in Arkansas.

Then I saw that Bailey's hand was raised, too. Bailey didn't usually ask stupid questions, so I wondered what she was up to. "Are we going to mail these?" she asked.

"Certainly."

"Well, what if you don't have a . . . an address?"

"Oh." Holt frowned. "Well, pick someone whom you *do* have an address for." She smiled then, that special smile she uses when she thinks she's come up with a smart idea.

"What if you don't have . . . any?"

Shut up, Bailey, shut up! I tried to send her signals. Already I could see Janie and Violet exchanging looks. *Just make up any address! What difference does it make?*

"Well . . . uh . . . why don't you just write something and talk to me afterwards?" Holt said.

I don't know if Bailey got my message, but she muttered, "I didn't mean *any* address for *anybody*." She bent over her paper.

She did mean she didn't know any relatives' address, I knew that. Man, imagine not knowing where anyone was, not even your parents. I wondered then if she'd been a foster kid her whole life. But she must have had parents to start out with.

When it was time to go out for recess, I went to the coat closet to get my Nerf football, but I stalled around inside the closet for a while, hoping I'd see Bailey. I wondered where she'd hid out yesterday. If she was going to do the same today, I wanted to find her. But when I came out of the closet, she wasn't in the classroom or the halls either, even though I looked for her. As I got near the stairs, I saw her. She was with Janie and Violet and Stephanie at the foot of the stairs. And from the look on her face, I knew just what was happening. They wanted to know why she didn't know where any of her relatives lived. I wondered then if she'd told anyone else that she was a foster kid.

I was at the top of the stairs when I saw them, and right away I flipped down the football. "Catch!" I said.

Bailey didn't seem to look up. But her hand shot up and she snatched the ball right out of the air. Major League reflexes.

Violet and Stephanie looked up and blinked, and Janie's hands flew up over her head and she ducked.

I gave them all one of my thousand-watt smiles, the kind I usually save for teachers. Then I said, "Run along, girls. You're supposed to be on the playground." Just like a teacher.

And, as if I *were* a teacher, they turned like good little sheep and headed for the door.

When they were gone, Bailey said, "Don't feel sorry for me, Pork-Rind." Her eyes were super-bright, though, and her voice came out like she was squeezing it past something in her throat.

I recognized that sound.

"I *do* feel sorry for you," I said.

She stuck out her chin and narrowed her eyes, just the way she had done on the steps earlier.

"And not for the reasons you think!" I added. "I feel sorry for you because you're so stupid."

"Yeah?"

"Yeah! You got a friend and you're not even smart enough to know it."

"Half a friend," she said. "*Outside* school."

"Half a friend is better than none."

"Not in my book."

Then, just like on the steps that morning, we were in a staring contest. Only this time I gave in.

"Okay, okay!" I said. "In school, too. But if you follow me around, I swear I'll flatten you."

She smiled, not quite her usual smile, but almost. "Don't worry, Big Shot," she said. "You think I want to hang around with you on the boys' playground? Those guys are creeps. How about I come over after school today?"

"But, you said . . ."

Then I guess it was the look on my face that made her laugh out loud. "What?" she said, laughing.

"You know. That . . ."

She laughed again. "See you this afternoon."

She ran out the side door toward the girls' playground.

8

AFTER SCHOOL that day, I went home, made a sandwich, and went out on the porch steps to wait for Bailey. Weird, but I was kind of looking forward to it. Much as I liked Brant, I did get kind of sick of him. He always wanted *me* to think up what we were going to do. With Bailey, I had an idea she might have some decent stuff in mind.

But even while I was looking forward to her coming over, this sickish feeling kept creeping over me, like something was expanding to fill the space where my stomach should be. Moving again, moving again, moving again. Just seeing the boxes in the kitchen, rearranged and partly packed up and all, made it all come back again. *Moving, moving, moving.* It was like a mean record round and round in my brain that I couldn't shut off.

"Shut up!" I said to it, out loud.

"I didn't even say anything yet," Bailey said.

I swung around. "How did you get here?" I sounded mean because I was embarrassed, having her hear me talk to myself. How had she gotten onto the porch behind me, anyway?

"I knocked on the back door," she said. She plopped down on the steps beside me. "You didn't answer and the door was open so I walked through the house." She gave me a funny look. "I didn't mean to scare you."

"You didn't scare me."

"Oh."

She was quiet for a minute, and then she said. "You moving again?"

"No, I'm not moving again!" What business of hers was it? And why did she have to bug me?

"You don't lie real good," she said. She added quickly, as if she was afraid I'd get mad, "There are boxes packed up in the kitchen, that's all."

"Well, we always have boxes packed up in the kitchen." It was true. We did. And I wasn't ready to tell her about it, even if it wasn't true.

"It's okay," she said, as if she already knew what I was thinking. "I don't tell everybody everything, either."

Then, just as suddenly, I changed my mind, and I felt like telling her, telling somebody, what was happening. "Pop's talking about moving again," I said.

"How come?"

"You mean you don't know?" I said it half-joking, but I was half-serious, too. I'd never met anyone who knew everybody's business the way she did.

"Nope," she said, seriously.

I broke off a piece of my sandwich and handed it to her.

We both ate quietly for a minute, and then I said, "It seems to me like Pop's only happy when we move. Like, we come to a new place and he loves it for a while. But then he's restless and mopey and right away, I know what's coming. And as soon as we're getting ready to move again, he's all happy again."

"Yeah?" She seemed to be listening carefully just the way Pop does.

"Yeah." I went on. "You know, it wasn't always like this. After I was born, you know I lived in the same house till I was *four*?"

She nodded.

"I still remember that house," I said. "I draw pictures of it sometimes. And I still remember my friends— Billy Friedman and Stan Whittaker. And Jessie. She was my friend."

"A *girl*?" Bailey grinned at me.

"Yeah, when you're little, it doesn't matter." I sort of rushed on because I didn't feel like getting into a fight with her over that. "But then, after my mom died, Pop couldn't stand the house. At least, that's what he said. He said it made him sad. So we moved, and then he was happy. Only he keeps on moving."

"Wow." Bailey sighed and pulled a strand of hair across her mouth and began sucking on it. "Do you hate it?" she said through her hair.

"I didn't when I was little. It was kind of fun. New places, and then, lots of times I'd be out of school for weeks at a time while we went from place to place, and that was fun. But after a while, you get sick of it. You make new friends and you have to start all over. Last couple years, every time he pulls out that atlas I get sick."

"You miss your mom?"

"Not so much anymore. But I know Pop does."

We were both quiet then for a long time. Bailey had

her head tipped back, looking up at the sky. I leaned my elbows back against the step and looked up, too. Clouds slipped from one fat shape into another—a giant's head, a man with a pointy beard, a goat on a mountain. Then they all slid together and melted away.

"Miss Holt's not married," Bailey said, and she sat up.

"What?"

"Miss Holt's not married." She smiled at me.

"So what?"

She grinned.

"Huh?" I wasn't even sure I had heard her right.

"I *said*, Miss Holt's not married."

"No way!" I said, because I suddenly began to have an idea what she was talking about. "Oh, no!"

"Why not?"

"It's berserk!" It was a word I'd never said till now, only read, but I suddenly liked the sound of it, so I said it again. "Miss Holt? Berserk!"

"Look." Bailey poked a finger into my chest like Miss Mitchell, my rotten fourth-grade teacher used to do when she was trying to make a point—only she'd poke so hard, she'd practically knock you over. Bailey didn't knock me over, but she poked hard, too. "He moves because he's sad."

Poke.

"He's sad because your mom died."

Poke.

"He needs another interest."

Big poke.

"Miss Holt!"

"Never," I said.

"Why not?"

"You don't know Pop. He's shy."

She shrugged. "So what? It happens all the time. Grown-ups have sex, too, you know."

"Who's talking about sex?"

"I am."

I shook my head. "It wouldn't work. Anyhow, how'd we get them together? What would we do? What would *they* do?"

"We'll figure it out."

"Berserk," I muttered again. Then I jumped up from the steps because I suddenly had a thought that was *really* berserk. "Do you know what that would mean if Pop married her?" I was practically shouting and I quickly looked around and lowered my voice, even though no one was there. "Her and Pop? Do you know what that would mean?"

She smiled, and I could see that she knew exactly what it would mean. She shrugged. "I could think of worse things. Miss Holt as your mother." She laughed. "Boy, wouldn't Brant be jealous."

"It's not funny," I said, and I sat down again. "I mean it. You are weird."

"Come on," she said. "Think about it."

"I did think about it."

"They don't have to actually get married. All they have to do is like each other—fall in love. Because if he's in love, he's not going to move away from here, is he? You said he moves because he's sad."

She looked at me like she was expecting an answer.

"You're weird" was my answer.

"You don't feel sad if you're in love." She said it like she had just settled something.

Well, that was probably true. "Maybe," I said.

"Okay," she said. "I'll think up something, a plan. Tonight. After I'm in bed. I'll call you tomorrow. Or maybe come over since we don't have school."

She stood up then. "Want to do something? Go exploring?"

"Yeah. Where?"

"I found a way to get on top of the A & P. It's pretty cool up there. And if you're not chicken, you can jump from there to the candy store. But you have to watch out that you don't slip in the cat poop."

"On *top* of the store?"

"Yeah. Cats live up there. Wanna go?"

"Sure."

I stood up too, and together we started for the stores. Bailey found a rock, and kicked it as we walked. I found one, too, and kicked mine. Pop and Miss Holt. It was a crazy idea. But maybe it was worth a try. From what I'd seen of Bailey so far, just maybe together we could make it work.

9

NEXT MORNING was Saturday, and I didn't wake up till ten-thirty. Pop wasn't home, because he works most Saturdays, especially in the fall. People always want to get their outdoor painting done before it gets cold. I was sitting in front of the TV watching cartoons, when the phone rang. Bailey.

"Can I come over?" she said.

"Sure."

"I got an idea."

"I'll bet you do," I said. I've never known anyone who has so many ideas.

"Meet you outside. Under the tree."

That was another thing I was beginning to learn about Bailey. She couldn't just meet me like regular people do, like at my house or at hers or at school. No, it had to be *behind* the paper stand, or on the steps of the school, or in back of the candy store, or, like now, under the tree.

"Okay," I said, and then, just as I was about to hang up, I remembered. "Hey, wait a minute!" I said. "What tree?"

"The big one. By the street in front of your house."

"Okay."

I finished my Froot Loops, and turned off the TV, and was waiting for her when she got there.

She plopped down on the grass next to me. "Getting them together is so easy you'll hardly believe it."

"Yeah?"

"Yeah. He invites her. She comes."

"He won't," I said. "I told you that yesterday. Pop's way too shy. He'd never invite her, no matter what I told him about her."

And then I saw that look she gets, and I said, "You wouldn't!" Even though I had a feeling she would. She was going to invite Miss Holt for Pop—without Pop even knowing about it.

"Nope," she said. "But you would." Then she saw *my* look and she added, "Think about it. You're a poet. You write these great things, so you could do it easy. . . ."

"What!" I stared at her.

"Well. . . ." She looked away. "Okay, so I looked through your notebooks in school. I looked in every-body's notebooks."

"You . . . You. . . ." Pork-Rind. Mosquito-Ass. Slug-Slime. Nothing seemed rotten enough. I didn't say anything.

She pulled up little bits of grass and sprinkled them onto her pants' legs. "Okay, so maybe I shouldn't have. Not yours, anyway. But I found some neat stuff in Stephanie's. Blackmail stuff. She picks her nose and wipes it in her notebook. Thousands of little buggers in there." She grinned at me.

I didn't think it was funny. I was still so mad I couldn't even speak.

"Well, how could I know we'd turn out to be friends?" Her face got red. "I had to be prepared. In case."

"I bet you did."

I thought about going back in the house and leaving her alone. But I just sat, not saying another word.

She was quiet for a while, too.

"They're nice poems," she said after a while, very quietly.

"Yeah?"

"Yeah."

More quiet.

"I liked 'Ode to Lord Alfred Bahr'," she said.

"You did?"

"Yeah. You still have him?"

I looked at her for the first time in a while. It was a poem I had written about Bahr, my bear. Blackmail?

"I have one, too," she said, and I knew she was talking about stuffed animals. She was handing me blackmail stuff if I wanted it. "I take him everywhere," she said. "But when I go someplace new, I leave him in the suitcase for a while."

She pulled up more grass and sprinkled it on herself again. "His name is Shakespeare," she said. "He writes stuff to me."

"*He* writes?"

"Well, you know. . . ."

"What kind of stuff? Poems?" I asked.

"No. He's lousy at poems." Her eyes got funny, sort of wistful. "But he writes good letters."

"Hmm."

"Look," she said. "Don't be mad. Okay?"

I made her wait a long, long minute. But then I said, "Okay."

"Okay!" she said. "Now about Miss Holt and—"

"Wait!" I said. "I told you, I don't think this is a good idea. I don't want Miss Holt for a . . ." I made a face. "Mother."

"They don't have to get married." She made a face too, as if I was unbelievably stupid. "I told you all that yesterday. Just fall in love and all that." She stuck her lower lip out and blew upward, trying to get grass bits off her nose. "Come on, yesterday you said maybe."

"It's still maybe."

"You want to stay here, don't you?"

She looked me over, and I looked back. I did want to believe her. If Pop fell in love, maybe he really would want to stay. Bailey made it seem so simple. She was so sure of herself.

"You sure?" I said, wanting to be convinced once more.

"I'm sure."

I sighed. "Okay."

"Okay!" she said. "So, you write the note, the invitation. Nice and formal, not too flowery or anything. And she'll send a note back. . . ."

"What if she doesn't send a note? What if she calls?"

"She won't. If he writes, she'll write."

"So what do we invite her to do?" I asked.

She flipped a piece of grass up into the air in front of her face, and then blew it away. "He invites her out to dinner."

I thought. "Pop doesn't have much money," I said.

Bailey flopped over, then sat up, picking bits of leaves and grass off her sweatshirt. "How about he invites her to his house—your house?"

"To dinner? *Pop?*" I had to laugh. "You never tasted his cooking."

"Okay, so we have to cook it ourselves." She dug around in her jeans' pockets and came up with the wrapping from some Hubba Bubba bubble gum, and a teeny bit of chewed up pencil. "Come on, let's go to the grocery store and see what a dinner will cost. We'll make a shopping list."

We both got up off the grass, and headed for the A & P. "It's gotta be special," I said. "Something really special."

"What can you cook?" Bailey asked.

"Eggs."

"No good," Bailey said.

"How about turkey?" I suggested.

"You ever cook one?"

"Nah, but I learn fast. Okay, turkey with stuffing, gravy, cranberry sauce. . . ."

Bailey was trying to write it all down. "Mashed potatoes," she muttered.

"Right. And sweet potatoes. Creamed onions."

Bailey looked up and made a face, but she wrote "O" down on the gum wrapper.

"Dinner rolls," I added.

Bailey nodded, then tried to write it on the wrapper, made a seriously ugly face and then threw the paper and the stubby pencil up into the air and walked on.

"Pumpkin pie, ice cream, coffee," she said. She used

her fingers to keep track of the items. "Grown-ups always like coffee."

"This sounds expensive," I said.

"So what?" She got this secret kind of smile on her face. "We'll find ways to make money. That's our next project."

Then we were at the A & P, and we headed right for the back where they have the frozen turkeys. We weren't actually buying the turkey and the rest of it, just pricing it and trying to keep the totals in our heads. We figured that fifteen dollars was about right, and we tried to keep it to that. But no matter how careful we were, it came to a lot more than that. The first time though, it was over thirty. So we settled on a smaller turkey, and one can of cranberry sauce instead of two, and one can of turkey gravy. We decided to forget about the onions. Still, the second time through it was over twenty-five dollars.

"It would work out just right if it weren't for the turkey," I said.

"Terrific," Bailey said. "A turkey dinner without the turkey." She looked at me then. "Unless we pretended to Holt that your pop's a vegetarian?"

I shook my head. "No. We got to really impress her. Big time. The way to impress somebody is to make them a turkey dinner. Come on, let's go through this again."

So once more we went around the store noting prices and sizes. We kept one small turkey—practically a chicken in disguise it was so small. A bag of potatoes. One can of cranberry sauce and one can of gravy. One can of sweet potatoes because it was cheaper than the real kind, and besides, neither of us knew how to cook the real kind.

We had just one dollar left, and no pumpkin pie, and no coffee, and no ice cream. So we decided we could use whatever coffee Pop had in the house, and we decided to make our own dessert—a cake, since we didn't know how to make pumpkin pie. A cake mix didn't even cost a dollar, so that was good. It would work out just fine.

When we went home, we began working on the letter to Miss Holt from Pop.

"What's her first name, do you know?" I asked Bailey.

"Lucinda," Bailey said.

"Lucinda! I don't want a Lucinda for a mother." Bailey kept saying it would never happen, but you couldn't tell.

"Don't worry about it!" she said for about the millionth time. "They're not going to actually get married. He's just going to fall in love. Now, should it be a poem or just regular?"

"A poem would be fun." I thought for a while. "How about this: Roses are red, violets are blue; come to my house, I'll make dinner for you."

Bailey shook her head.

I shrugged.

We both thought for a while, and then Bailey said, "How about this: Violets are blue, roses are red; eat up my dinner, you'll fall down dead."

"That's more like it," I said. "Especially if Pop really did cook it."

And then we filled up pages and pages of junk and silly stuff before we came up with what we both knew was just exactly right. We had to eliminate poems completely. Dignified. And simple. Dignified was Bailey's idea. Simple was mine. So this is what we finally wrote:

"Dear Miss Holt—" (we decided that "Lucinda" was much too personal for Pop to use when he didn't even know her yet)—"I would be most gratified if you would dine with me some Saturday night soon. R.S.V.P."

Perfect.

So while I made some peanut butter sandwiches, Bailey ran back to her house to steal some stationery from her foster mom. Pop didn't have anything at all to use.

In just minutes, Bailey was back, on her bike this time, with two sheets of paper and two blue envelopes tucked inside her sweatshirt. It was a good thing she brought two sheets, because we wasted one before we got it just right. Bailey wrote it, in case Miss Holt recognized my handwriting. Even if she thought Pop's handwriting was kind of weird, she'd never think to connect it with Bailey. Then we sealed up the envelope, and it was ready to go on Monday morning.

10

I SHOULD HAVE KNOWN, though, that Bailey wouldn't wait till Monday morning to come up with more ideas. I was barely awake Sunday when she was pounding on the door. *Pounding*.

"Shush!" I said, as I opened the door.

She came in and looked around. "Your pop still asleep?"

"Yup."

She followed me into the kitchen. "You know how in fairy tales bears come out of the woods and beat on cottage doors?" she asked.

"No," I said.

"You were a deprived child," she answered. "You should have read fairy tales. Well, they do. I was pounding on the door pretending I was a bear."

"Naturally," I said, and I made a face at her. "I always do that."

She made a face back.

I went to the cabinet and got out the Froot Loops and two bowls and spoons and brought them to the table.

Bailey got the milk from the refrigerator and we both sat down and poured cereal.

While I ate, I looked at Bailey, and couldn't help feeling a little surprised. She seemed so . . . clean. Not that she's ever really dirty, but always kind of scruffy. That morning though, her hair was clipped up in a barrette, and it was brushed so hard it shone. Her eyes seemed even bigger with her hair brushed up like that. She was wearing the same old jeans, but a sweater I'd never seen before. I didn't like it much—it was that nylon stuff that gives me chills to touch. But it did fit her better than those enormous sweatshirts she usually wore.

She must have noticed how I was looking at her, because she put down her spoon, and pulled the barrette out of her hair. She shook her head so hard that her hair fell forward over her face again.

"Church," she said.

"Oh."

"Wait'll you hear my plan." She picked up her spoon.

"Uh-oh."

"No, you're gonna love it. We'll make big money. *Big* money. We can spend fifty dollars on this dinner if we want!"

"Yeah?"

"Yeah," she said. "A pet wash! We'll wash anything—dogs, cats, birds, horses. Anything."

"Gimme a break. Who washes birds? Or cats?"

"Nobody, that's the point. The whole world's got pets, and everybody's pets get dirty, but nobody wants to wash them." She pointed her spoon at me, and milk dripped from it onto the table. She made little swirls in it with her pinky finger. "And that's where we come in. We do it for them, and they pay us."

"Cats scratch," I said. "And dogs bite."

She sighed. "That's what I like. Enthusiasm."

"Well, I'm still half-asleep." I tried to think of one good thing to say about her idea. "I like horses. It would be fun to wash a horse."

"Yeah," she agreed. "But where're we going to find a horse around here?"

"Horses, horses," I said softly, thinking. Nope. I couldn't think of a single horse or anyplace I'd even seen one. This wasn't a city like Chicago or New York, but it wasn't country, either. Stamford was just a small city, like lots of others I've been in. There wasn't even enough grass around to feed a goat, much less a horse. I shook my head.

"Okay, then," she said. "We'll have to settle for dogs and cats. It's not hard once you learn."

"You ever done it?"

"No."

"Then how do you know?"

"I know, that's all. Same as you know how to cook a turkey. You can learn anything."

"How much you plan to charge?"

"Five dollars each pet."

"Five dollars!" Now I *was* interested. "Is this how you got the five bucks to pay me when I swallowed Goldie?"

"I told you, I never did this before." She grinned. "I got that from babysitting for six kids at once."

"You think people will really pay that much to get their pets washed?"

"Why not? You take 'em to a pet grooming place or

a vet and they charge twenty at least. They'll be glad to pay us five."

"Okay," I said. "But we'll have to advertise. And if this is a *real* paid job, I mean, really professional, we got to do it right. Think we ought to practice first?"

"Yeah." She looked around. "You got a dog or cat?"

"Nope. Do you?"

"Nope."

"Hmm."

"I know where I can get a cat, though," she said. "Mrs. Vogel next door has about a billion cats."

"Are you sure about this cat stuff? I thought cats washed themselves."

"I'm sure." She pushed her hair back out of her eyes. "Once I lived with this lady called Mrs. Hughes. She was the fattest person you ever saw. I called her Mrs. Huge. She must have had a hundred cats, and they used to get mites—creepy black stuff in their ears. She had to wash it out." Bailey shivered. She let her hair fall forward again and picked up her spoon and began to eat.

"Yuck. I'm not sure I want to do that."

"Five bucks," Bailey said through her Froot Loops.

"Yeah, yeah."

"This Mrs. Huge?" Bailey said. "Her cats got huge, too. Ever notice that? Pets get just like their owners. Or the other way around."

She looked up at me. "So, want me to kidnap one of Mrs. Vogel's cats and we'll practice on it?"

"Mrs. Vogel going to be mad?"

"How's she going to know? All she'll know is she let out a dirty cat and got a clean one back in."

That seemed to make sense. "Okay," I said. "You go do that and I'll get the stuff ready. We'll need soap and rags and a bucket, and—"

"Gloves," Bailey said. "Heavy gloves. Like gardening stuff."

I nodded. "I'll look."

We both stood up and took our bowls to the sink. Then Bailey left to catch a cat, but before she went, I said, "Listen, try for a dog, okay? I'm not crazy about this cat idea."

"I'll try," she said. "But I don't know where."

After she'd gone, I went out to the garage. We only rented the house, and the owners had left all kinds of junk out there. I found a plastic bucket and one pair of gardening gloves—but just one pair. Bailey and I would just have to take turns. I went back to the kitchen to look for soap. What kind of soap did you use to wash dogs and cats? Nothing like Mr. Clean because it might be too strong, hurt their skins or fur. Dish washing soap might be okay. It bubbled up a lot and it didn't hurt your hands. But when I looked under the kitchen sink we were all out of dish washing liquid. Bar soap? The fur might stick to it. Still, I didn't see any other choice, so that's what I took—a fat white bar of Ivory soap. I went outside with it and with the bucket and rags and gloves and waited for Bailey.

In just a few minutes, I saw her riding down the middle of the street on that huge old bike of hers. She was riding no hands, just balancing the bike and weaving back and forth across the road, but all wobbly as if she was about to fall over. Both hands were pressed into the basket of the bike.

When she saw me, she shouted, "Quick! Come here!" She skidded to a stop, both hands on the twisting, furry thing that was trying to fight its way out of her hold. "Where are the gloves?" she called.

"Here!" I threw them to her.

"What am I supposed to do with those? Put them on—hurry!—help me. Ow!"

I picked up the gloves and put them on.

Mrow! Mrow! It was a cat in the basket and it howled like it was being murdered.

"Listen here, cat, listen here, cat," Bailey kept saying. But the cat sure wasn't listening.

Mrow!

"Hurry up, will you?" Bailey said. "Just take him. Talk nice to him."

She was pressing down so hard on the cat's back that it was almost flat against the basket.

"Nice cat," I murmured.

Mee . . . eee . . . row! The cat screamed like I had just run it over with my bike.

"Oh, shut up," I said. I got my hands under its belly and lifted it out of the basket and away from Bailey's hold. It hung stiffly from my hands, its legs marching up and down in the air while I held it away from my body.

When it stopped clawing the air, very carefully I brought it closer to me. It was still stiff, and its tail was twitching, but at least it didn't scratch.

Bailey put her hand in her mouth and sucked on it noisily. "Stupid cat. Scratched me."

"Well, I told you to get a dog."

"Yeah? Where? And did you ever try to put a dog in the basket of your bike?"

I shrugged.

Together we went around the house to where I had the bucket underneath the outside faucet. While I held the cat, Bailey filled the bucket and dropped in the bar of soap.

I looked down at the cat in my hands. It was black and white and had soft, nice-looking fur. It really didn't look at all dirty. But since it was just practice, I guessed it didn't matter.

"Is this Mrs. What's-her-name's cat?" I asked.

"Yup. It was asleep on her step." Bailey smiled at me. "Boy, was it surprised. It never had a bike ride before." She looked into the bucket and swished the water around with her hands. There were no soap suds or bubbles at all.

"Think this stuff will work?" she asked.

"Why not? It works on people."

"Yeah?" She sounded doubtful.

"Doesn't matter," I said. "It's only practice."

"How do we do it?" Bailey was eyeing me and the cat like we were zoo creatures.

"I thought you knew," I said. "How did Mrs. Monster do it?"

"Mrs. Huge," she muttered. But she still looked puzzled.

"What difference?" I said. But I decided it was time for me to take charge since she obviously didn't know what to do next. And the cat was marching in the air again. It wasn't going to wait much longer. "Okay," I said. "This is what we do. You hold the bucket. I hold the cat. Back to me, paws facing the side of the bucket. That way it can't scratch. I dip him in. You swish water over his back. Then we dry him up. And . . . clean cat. We can let him go."

Mad, crazy cat bones.

She nodded and moved over a little, making room for me in front of the bucket.

"Here goes," I said.

Slowly, carefully, I lowered the cat into the water.

Instantly, it became a maniac cat. It let out a howl that was a combination roar and a scream and began scrabbling up the side of the bucket like it was on fire.

I was trying to hold it down, and Bailey was madly splashing water over its back. And all over me and her. Water was in my face and on my shirt and jeans, and I was almost as wet as the cat.

I couldn't help laughing, and Bailey was almost hysterical.

That maniac cat was shrinking. As its fur got wetter and wetter, all the fluff was gone and all you could see was its bones. Little tiny cat bones.

Mad, crazy cat bones.

In another instant, it had freed itself from my hands, turned over the bucket, and was clawing its way out of the water. And then it was gone, just a streak of wet fur that disappeared around the corner of the house.

Bailey and I collapsed on the ground.

11

THERE ARE ALWAYS about a million kids bringing in notes in the mornings, so on Monday, when I slid the blue envelope with the invitation onto Miss Holt's desk, she hardly noticed. She just left it there with all the others until attendance time when she reads all the notes together.

But after she read it, she definitely changed. Or was I imagining it? I noticed that she kept rereading the notes, and I thought she was reading one in particular. Was it the blue one? It had to be.

I stretched out of my desk as far as I dared, but I couldn't see. I got up and went to the pencil sharpener so I could sort of look casually over her desk—not too obvious. Still I couldn't tell. She had a mess of papers up there.

But maybe I was right about her being happy, because Bailey thought so, too. At break time, when Miss Holt took her thermos and coffee mug out in the hall, Bailey came over to my desk and did her thumbs-up sign. "She loves it! Notice how excited she is?"

"You think so?" I said. "Me, too!"

"We got it made," Bailey said, and she went back to her desk.

The whole day went by and Holt didn't give me a note for Pop or say anything at all about it. At three o'clock, when I felt as if I'd burst, when it didn't look as if Holt had written anything or was about to give me anything, she called my name just as everyone as leaving. "Kevin?" she said. "Would you stay for a moment?"

I could feel Bailey's eyes. Magnets clamped to my back. I didn't dare look at her. But I knew where I'd find her when I finally got out of there—by the front steps, waiting to read Miss Holt's answering note.

When the classroom was empty, Miss Holt pulled a chair away from the front row and set it up near her desk. "Sit here, Kevin," she said.

I came up and sat, my heart hammering blows at the center of my chest.

"Umm, Kevin, you gave me a note this morning."

"Yes, Ma'am." Whenever I get nervous, I talk the way I used to talk when I lived in Alabama, and everybody had to say "Ma'am or "Sir" to the teachers and all the grown-ups.

"From your father?" she said.

I swallowed. "Yes, Ma'am."

"Um, do you know what was in the note?"

"No, Ma'am. Is something wrong? Did I do something?" Yeah, that was the way to go. Let her think I thought I was in trouble, and she'd never guess the truth.

She shook her head. "No, Kevin, nothing's wrong. You're sure you didn't read what your father wrote?"

I blinked at her. "I'm sure." That wasn't a lie, since Pop hadn't written it.

She nodded, and then she looked so puzzled and worried that I suddenly thought I understood. I even felt a little sorry for her. She was going to reject Pop, that's what, and she didn't know how to do it.

No problem, since Pop wouldn't even know he'd been rejected. That made me feel as if I was going to laugh, and I could feel my face cracking up on me. I made the hardest effort I've ever made in my life to stiffen it up again.

For a long time Miss Holt stared off toward the back of the room, not speaking. She had one bright pink fingernail set in the dimple in the center of her chin. She really was awfully pretty for a teacher.

"Your mom?" she said after a minute, still not looking at me. "I think I know from school records that you don't have a mom living. . . ."

"Oh, no! I don't have a mom! Not anymore, anyway." I could feel my face getting hot. "You don't think Pop would. . . ."

Oh, hell. I did it.

But it was probably all right, because she laughed right out loud. "So you did read it?"

"Oh, no, Ma'am! No! It's just that . . . well, you know . . . I mean, Pop talks about you. . . ."

She got this really funny look on her face. "He's never met me, has he? Except maybe at PTA early this fall. And I don't know that we ever talked." She looked at me. "Did we?"

"Oh, yes," I said, and I tried to copy the look that Bailey uses when she talks to teachers—the one she calls her "sincere" look. "Yes, you did."

They hadn't, I remembered. Pop's way too shy, and

I remembered that he'd acted like he wanted to talk to her, but he just looked at all the exhibits and stuff, and then we went home.

"We did?" Holt said again.

"Yup, you did. Pop remembers." The best acting job I've ever done in my life. I looked right in her face, and I didn't even blush. I could tell.

Holt nodded, frowning, and I could tell she was trying to remember. Then she smiled at me, a funny smile that I couldn't understand. Or could I? She was thinking about being my mother!

Bailey, you and your stinkin' ideas!

"Can I go now?" I asked.

"*May* I go now?" she repeated, but sort of absent-mindedly. Then she kind of shook her head and looked directly at me, and her voice was more direct. "Tell your father that I'll . . . speak to him soon."

"Oh, no! Don't do that! I mean, don't speak to him. I mean, he's terribly shy, especially on the phone. . . . I mean that's why he sends notes." All confused. If Bailey had been there, she'd have been disgusted. "I mean," I said, one final effort, "he's really shy. Like *really* shy."

"Like his son?"

"What?"

She stood up, and I stood and backed toward the door.

She smiled. "Tell him I'll be in touch."

I turned and raced for the stairs.

Outside, Bailey was waiting for me by the steps, and she stuck out her hand as I came through the door. "Where is it?" she said.

"There isn't any 'it.' She didn't give me anything."

"Well, what'd she say? Is she gonna go?"

"She didn't say. She just thought for a long time, and she asked me stupid questions, like about my mom, and I got all weird, and I think she knew. . . ."

Bailey looked sick. "Knew that you wrote the note?"

"No. But she knew that I knew what was in the note."

Bailey shrugged, and made one of those huge sighs of relief. "Big deal! Every kid reads every note that parents write. Especially if they're sealed up. Teachers expect it."

"Yeah, but you know what else? She said she'd call and—"

"Okay, okay!" She interrupted me, super-excited. "That means she'll go!"

"Listen!" I glared at her. "I had to talk her out of calling. And what if she calls anyway? Besides. . . ." I looked at her. "How do you know that means she'll go?"

"Easy! She wouldn't call if she wasn't going to go. She just wouldn't answer the note or call or anything." She twisted a piece of hair round and round her finger, then pulled it across her mouth and sucked on it. Through the hair, she mumbled, "What excuse did you give to keep her from calling?"

"Told her Pop was too shy."

She spit out her hair. "Good answer."

"But what if she calls anyway?"

"No biggie. You just answer the phone every time it rings."

"Oh, great. I can just see it: races . . . from bathtub to kitchen . . . grabs phone from Pop's hand . . . acts *real* cool . . . says, 'No, Miss Holt, my pop's not here' . . . while Pop stares, wide-eyed. . . ."

Bailey was grinning. "You worry too much. We got what we wanted. She thinks your pop's really interested. All we have to do now is sit back and wait. *And* come up with a plan for making money so we can afford the dinner."

"Like cat washing?" I said it real sarcastically, but she didn't seem to notice.

"No," she said. "I have a new plan. It's not all worked out yet but I should have it figured out by tomorrow. I'll tell you then."

"Great," I said, but I didn't even try to sound sarcastic anymore. I was just relieved that it would be tomorrow before I heard the new plan. I'd had enough of Bailey's plans for one day.

But all the way home, I worked on mapping out my own plan—how to take the fastest bath or shower on record; how to do my homework while hanging over the phone; how to do everything while being not more than a few feet away from the telephone. Because if Holt called, and I wasn't there to handle it, all our careful plans would be blown away. And I didn't even want to think what that would mean.

12

My FIRST THOUGHT when I got home that day was that we had company. A strange car was in front of the house. But who? We hardly knew anybody. And then I realized what it was—Pop's new car—and that familiar sensation of a knotted fist came back to my stomach, because now, for sure, we'd be going.

Yet I couldn't help feeling curious about the car, and slowly I walked up to where it was parked at the curb. It was an old Chevy, the kind you hardly ever see anymore. Even though it was old and dented up, it shone like somebody had really worked on it. The chrome part especially was so shined up that I could see my reflection in it. And it had the new tires Pop had been talking about, the tread so deep I could stick my fingers in it. It was a cool-looking old car, and I pictured myself riding to school in it, getting out in front of the school, real casual-like with everybody staring at me. And then I pictured myself going somewhere else in it—to Oklahoma—and I felt like bursting into tears. But I wouldn't. Not with Pop watching me from the front window, as I was sure he was doing, enjoying me enjoying his car.

I opened the car door and slid inside.

"Nice, huh?"

It was Pop. He had come out of the house and stood beside the car, running his hand over it really softly like it was a person. "Like it?"

"Yeah. When'd you get it?"

He laughed. "About fifteen minutes ago. Traded in the old heap. Want a ride?"

"Sure."

He turned back to the house to get his keys. He'd been wearing an apron, and as he went, he untied it. Just briefly, I wondered what he'd been dreaming up for supper.

While he was gone, I looked over the inside of the car. It was all black plastic—dashboard, controls and all, even the seat covers. The elastic band that held one of the covers in place had slipped a little on one side, and I could see the plaid seat underneath, the stuffing springing out a little bit. I tugged the cover back into place.

I fingered the controls, the knobs, the radio. Was it a stereo?

Pop came out without his apron on and slid into the seat beside me. He put the key in the ignition, and said, "Now watch this."

Very slowly, the seat beneath me started to rise up higher, while it tilted me backward at the same time.

"Hey, that's okay!" I said.

"And that's not all." Pop flicked a switch, and I heard a loud, clicking sound.

"Yeah?" I said.

"Try your door," Pop answered.

I tried it, but it wouldn't open.

"Automatic locks," Pop said. "One switch, and every door in the car is locked. And now, this is the best part."

I watched as he did something else, and suddenly the steering wheel began to lift and tilt toward him.

He grinned at me. "How's that?"

"Cool, really cool. Okay, so we going to sit at the curb all day?"

Pop laughed, then very slowly he inched the car backward, then forward and out into the street. He went so slowly that it seemed like he had had his driver's license for about fifteen minutes.

While he drove, I fiddled around with the radio. I tried every station, but nothing came out except static.

"I know," Pop said, though I hadn't said anything. "It needs a little adjusting. I could tell that myself. But we'll fix it before we go."

Go. Before we go.

"When are we going?" I asked, and my voice came out smaller that I had intended.

"Well, soon. We'll talk about it after supp—Ohmigosh, the soup!"

He slammed on the brakes right there in the middle of the street, and then began negotiating a turn. The car was so long that he had to go backward and forward and backward and forward about five times, and still it wasn't turned around.

Behind us, people was honking horns like mad.

Pop kept muttering, "How could I forget the soup, how could I forget the soup?" He didn't even seem to hear the horns and the people shouting at us.

He looked at me once and grinned kind of sheepishly. "So what's a burned pot?" he said, but I thought he looked a little anxious.

By the time we got fully turned around, it seemed like every car in the city was honking at us.

"It's okay," Pop kept saying to the other drivers as we passed going in the opposite direction. "It's okay." He acted like he had to calm them down, and didn't even look upset at some of the things that were shouted at him.

Because it was five o'clock, there was lots of traffic and it took about fifteen minutes for us to get home. Pop jerked the car to a stop in front of the house. We both jumped out.

Pop sniffed. "Can't smell anything yet." And then we both ran for the house.

Pop got to the door first and opened it. I almost fell over backward with the smell. It was sickening. Overpowering and gross.

Pop hurried to the stove, grabbed the pot, and pulled it off the burner.

I held the door wide to let the smell out. The stink would never go away, I was sure of it. We'd probably *have* to move now, just to get away from it.

"Hey, it didn't burn!" Pop said. "It's okay."

"It didn't what?"

"Didn't burn. It's fine. Just fine."

"You mean it's *supposed* to smell that way?"

"Well, I don't know how it's supposed to smell." Pop sounded a little hurt. "I've never made it before."

Good, I thought. *Hope you never make it again*. But I didn't say it out loud. "What is it?" I asked.

"Green soup."

"Green soup?" I waved the door back and forth hard to stir up a breeze. "Green, like pea soup?"

"No, like greens. You know, spinach, lettuce, cabbage, all that. I've been reading that greens are good for you." He brought the pot over for me to look in. "Brussels sprouts, too," he said proudly. "How does it look?"

He stirred it around with a big wooden spoon, and if I hadn't known what was in it, and it hadn't smelled like that, I think I might have said that it looked good. It was an interesting green color, with globs like little flowers floating on top. The brussels sprouts?

"I even got asparagus," Pop said. "But they had to come out of a can."

"But why'd you put them all in together?" I asked.

"Greens are good for you," Pop said. He took the pot and put it back on the stove on the burner.

Just like Pop! All the way. I began to think that this might be the first night ever that I didn't eat what he cooked.

"You hungry?" Pop asked.

"Not really. It's awfully early. How come you're home so early anyway?"

"The car. As soon as they told me it was ready, I left. Had to get my hands on that baby."

"Yeah." I didn't look at him. *Oklahoma, here we come.*

I picked up my books from where I had dropped them on the table when we ran in. "I'm going to do some homework," I said, and I started for my room.

"I'll call you when dinner's ready," he said.

I went to my room and shut the door. I didn't care if Holt called now. Let her. We were going anyway. It was all over now. We had no more time. No time for plans.

No time for Pop to fall in love. No time for anything. I had to fight back tears. I'd have to get in that stupid car without a radio and drive, and drive, and drive. . . .

I yanked open a desk drawer and took out an old notebook and began to write. Anything. Poems, anything. I would not cry. Pop would know. As soon as we sat down to dinner, he'd know with one look at me.

But I didn't write poems. I drew about a thousand pictures of airplanes with gunshots, streaks of fire going through them, and then I crumpled them all up and drew some more. I shot up all the planes, stabbing them so hard with my pencil that I made holes in the paper.

And then Pop was knocking at my bedroom door, and when he opened it, he had the car keys in his hand. "Pizza tonight," he said.

I just looked at him.

"I tasted it," he said.

I couldn't help laughing, and we both went out to the car.

We were waiting for the pizza to come, when Pop said, "We won't go for a while yet."

"We won't what?"

"We won't go yet."

He reached across the table and took my hand. We both grabbed at the Coke that spilled over, sending ice and Coke and melted water all over me. But I hardly noticed. *We weren't going yet.* He said it. When then?

"When?" I asked out loud.

"Oh, a few weeks maybe? I have this job to finish. It's a big house."

He was lying. I knew it. He wasn't looking at me, even though he had taken my hand again.

He rubbed my hand back and forth with his thumb. "Would Thanksgiving be all right? That would give you a little more time."

So he did know. Even though I had tried to keep it from him, he knew.

But he needed to move! He needed to or else he'd be sad. Unless . . . unless. . . . Unless Bailey was right. But, could we get him to fall in love that fast?

"How long till Thanksgiving?" I asked. "A month or so?"

Pop nodded. "About that."

"That's okay then," I said. And I meant it. I pulled my hand out of Pop's and began mopping up the ice that was still sitting in my lap. A month. It could work. With Bailey, we'd *make* it work.

"On my birthday," Pop said. "It'll be my birthday present to me."

I looked up and Pop was smiling at me, really relaxed. When I'd said it was okay to go at Thanksgiving I'd meant it, and he could tell. And it *was* okay, because it would never happen. But then I began to get that lumpy feeling inside my chest that I got whenever we talked about moving. Suppose he didn't fall in love? Suppose she wouldn't even come and have dinner with him?

She had to, that was all. I'd have to get together with Bailey and we had to make it happen. Up till now, I'd thought Bailey was a little crazy. Maybe she was. Maybe we both were. But crazy or not, this was a plan we had to make work.

13

I SAT ALONE on the front steps after we came home from the pizza place that night. I had taken the telephone from the kitchen table, and pulled it as close to the door as it would reach, just in case Holt called. Even though it was October, it was warm, and the front steps made a good private place to think when it was almost dark.

Less than a month. I had checked it on my calendar. Bailey and I had a lot of work to do. Could we do it? Could we make it happen? Would Holt possibly agree to come to dinner?

Out on the street, a car was coming, and in its head-lights I could see the yellow reflectors of a bike coming from the opposite direction. The bike stopped in front of the house and Bailey hopped off. Even in the near-dark I could tell it was her.

"Hey!" she said when she saw me. She jumped up the two steps and sat down beside me. "Wait'll you hear this plan."

"It better be good," I said. "And it better be quick."

"Yeah?"

"Yeah. Pop's made up his mind. Thanksgiving."

"Oh, wow." She was quiet for a minute, and then she sighed. "Okay, so we have to do it fast. No problem. Now listen, we need money, right?"

"I'm not sure," I said. I wasn't sure. I wasn't at all sure that this was going to work. How did we know that Holt would really agree to come?

Bailey smacked both hands against the steps. "Geez, are you a pain! Of course we need money because of course Holt's coming to supper. Now don't be a jerk. Listen to this plan. It's much better than pet washing. How about a school paper?"

"For money?"

"Yeah, for money."

"How you going to make money on a school paper?"

"You sell it, child. Sell, sell, sell."

"Who'd buy it?" I asked. "School papers are boring. There's nothing going on in a school that's any fun at all."

"Wanna bet? We could make it a paper that everybody wants to read—tell stuff about the teachers and all. Like how Miss Holt goes out with Mr. Luparello—"

"Does she really?" I looked at Bailey. "Really? But he's so old. And what about Pop?"

Bailey groaned. "Geez, are you weird. No, *he* doesn't and *she* doesn't. That was just an example. But we could find out lots of things, true things, and then write them up."

"And make money on it?"

"Yup."

"Hmm. How much, you figure?"

"Well, if there's three hundred kids in the school, and

we sell the papers for ten cents each, that's thirty bucks. We could have lobster for that."

I couldn't help saying it just one more time. "You sure she's going to come?"

"I'm sure. Now, get this. We persuade Holt to give us class time to do this project. So besides making money on it, we get out of class work at the same time."

"Think she'll go for it?"

"We'll work on a sales pitch." She looked at me. "So whatta you think?"

I grinned at her. "Well, it beats swallowing three hundred flies." And then I began to get some ideas. A paper might be just the thing for. . . .

"So," I said, real casually. "How about we have some columns, you know, sports, news from the different classes." I hesitated just a bit. "A poetry column."

"Columns isn't a bad idea," Bailey said. "But I don't know about the poetry part." She said *poetry* the same way she'd been saying *cats* for the last few days—a sort of shiver in her voice.

I gave her a shove, and she fell off the two steps.

She scrambled back up. "Okay, you get to do the poetry part. But I get to be the class reporter. I find out everything that's going on. Man, do I know some good stuff already."

"Like what?"

"Like that Mr. Luparello rides a tricycle."

"A what?"

"A tricycle. One of those grown-up things with the fat wheels."

"How do you know?"

"I was in his cellar."

"You were? Why? Why'd he invite you in there?"

She gave me one of those how-could-anybody-be-so-dumb looks. "He didn't invite me. I snuck in. It stinks in there. All moldy and there's toads there, too. And worms. Wettest cellar in town. But he's got some interesting stuff. I rode the tricycle."

She leaned back against the steps, her elbows out, her fists against her chest, legs stuck out in front of her. "Vroom!" she said softly under her breath. But she looked more like she was riding a motorcycle, instead of a grown-up's tricycle.

She grinned at me. "It was squeaky so I had to get off. And I know stuff about other people. Like Janie."

"What about her?"

"She's a wimp."

"Big deal. Everybody knows that."

She grinned. "Not everybody knows that she sucks her thumb and rubs her hair at the same time. She goes in the bathroom, locks herself in a stall, and sucks her thumb like crazy."

"How do you know?"

Again she grinned. "How do you think I know?"

"Oh," I said.

"Don't worry," she said. "I never go in the boys' bathroom."

"But none of that is stuff you can put in a school paper."

"Maybe, maybe not. But maybe we could use some of it for blackmail. Tell people that we'll put stuff in the paper if they don't promise to buy a copy."

I looked at her. "Would you really do that?" I asked slowly.

She shrugged. "Maybe." Then she sighed. "Probably not. Depends how bad I needed the money. And we are going to need money."

I wasn't going to say it again—*are you sure we're going to need money for a dinner?*—because I was beginning to sound like a wimp myself. But when Bailey spoke, it was she who asked the question I was thinking.

"Think she'll really do it? Agree to come?" Bailey asked. It was the first time she hadn't sounded absolutely sure.

"Don't you?" I said.

"Yeah. I was just asking."

But she didn't sound sure at all.

"I have the telephone right there inside the door," I said. "Just in case she calls. You know, I think she might . . . not call, but I think she might come."

"Course she will!" Bailey sat up straight, and didn't sound at all as if she had had any doubt in her voice before. "She's gonna send a note. You know how teachers are. They love to see their own handwriting. She'll send a note and say how 'thrilled and delighted' she'll be to join him for dinner. You just wait."

She took a piece of gum out of her pocket, broke it in two, and handed one half to me and put the other part in her mouth. She blew a bubble as big as her face, then crossed her eyes and watched the bubble spring a leak and slowly sink in till it rested on her cheeks. Then she picked the gum off and put it back in her mouth again. "Now we gotta plan," she said. "We got to talk Holt into this, and get permission for the school mimeo or whatever. And we got to be sure to tell her this is a onetime thing, right? I mean, we're not going to be writing a school paper every week or month or anything."

"Course not," I said.

Bailey shrugged. "Well, you know teachers. Once they get you hooked, they think they have you forever."

"I think we better meet *really* early tomorrow," I said. "Like seven o'clock. Because we have to plan the best sales pitch anyone's ever had." I had to laugh, because I suddenly had a funny thought. "Holt has to cooperate to help us make money to make her a dinner that Pop doesn't even know he's invited her to."

"Right," Bailey said. "We've cooked up the best plan anyone's ever had. And it's gonna work, too." She sounded really convinced again, and I was beginning to believe it, too.

Tomorrow was sure to be a good day.

14

NEXT MORNING, as planned, we met by the newsstand at seven o'clock. We had to have just the right words to say to persuade Holt, so we went over and over what we'd say:

There's so much going on that's important in this school . . . (Oh, barf). . . . And somebody should be reporting it, telling people, letting kids take home the news . . . (Barf, super-barf). . . . And Miss Holt, wouldn't it be great if the fifth graders could be the ones to do this? I mean, we're next to oldest in this school, and the sixth graders think they're such hot stuff . . . (No, maybe we shouldn't say that exactly). . . . Okay, so the sixth graders think they're such hot sh— . . . (No, maybe we shouldn't say *that* exactly). . . . So the sixth graders think they're the only ones with any good ideas in this school, but here's our own idea, one we could do, and we're offering it because we think it would benefit the school . . . (Don't get carried away, not even Miss Holt is that dumb). . . . Okay, we're offering because . . . (Hey, how about being honest? That always throws a teacher). . . . Because we like to write and besides, it would get us out of some class work. And it's only just this one time. We're just going to do this one issue, so it won't take *that* much time. . . .

We went over and over it, each of us putting in a thought, a sentence or two, until we thought we had it exactly right. By eight o'clock, we were sitting side-by-side at our desks, waiting for Holt when she arrived. And both of us wondering if she'd have an answer for Pop.

At first, she seemed surprised to see us waiting there, that same kind of look on her face that she'd had that morning when I was in early trying to save Goldie's life. But she just smiled at us, that nice kind of smile she has, and I wondered if Pop would like her.

"Good morning," she said quietly. "You both look bright and fresh this morning."

Bailey didn't answer, not even good morning. I'd noticed that it's never a good idea to be too nice to Bailey. She just clams up.

"Good morning," I said for both of us, and I kicked Bailey under the desk.

Miss Holt put her things down on her desk, sat down and opened her grade book. While she sipped from the coffee cup she had brought with her, she made a few marks in the grade book. Or was it the note to Pop she was writing? I looked at Bailey, questioning, but she just shrugged.

After a minute, without looking up, Miss Holt said, "Anything special?"

I looked at Bailey.

"Not really special," Bailey said. "But we had sort of an idea."

Together then, we told her our plan for the school

paper. We left out the part about why we wanted the money. In fact, we didn't even tell her how much we planned to charge, except to say that we were charging for it and we'd figure out how much later.

Miss Holt listened to us, a serious look on her face, like she was considering what we were talking about. But after a while, I noticed that she was frowning hard and chewing on her lip, that thing that grown-ups do when they're trying not to laugh.

Bailey noticed, too, and she got grim-looking, but she plowed on, ending with the thing we'd planned. "Besides," she said, very matter-of-factly, "it will get us out of class work."

Miss Holt laughed right out loud. She didn't even try not to.

I wasn't sure if that was a good sign or not, but Bailey was grinning.

"I have to hand it to you," Miss Holt said after a minute. "I thought you were trying to con me, but you're awfully honest. I appreciate that." And she laughed again, and got that young look, and I thought, *No wonder Brant thinks he's in love with you. Maybe Pop will fall in love with you, too.*

But Holt had suddenly gotten serious again. "All right. But remember this: I'm going to leave the paper completely up to you. You'll be responsible for the whole thing—news, everything. All I'm going to do is help if you need something. And I'll have to see the paper before it's copied."

"Okay!" We both said it together.

"How much time do we get out of class to do it?" Bailey asked.

"How much time do you need?" Miss Holt asked quietly.

"Two hours a day," Bailey said immediately.

I almost choked.

Miss Holt looked right into Bailey's eyes. "For how long?" she asked.

"Three . . ." Bailey hesitated just a part of a second. She opened her mouth around a word, then seemed to re-form it around a different word. "Three . . . days," she said.

I'd have sworn she'd been about to say three weeks.

"Maybe four," Bailey added quickly. "It's only this one time. One issue."

"I'll give you a week," Miss Holt said.

She nodded at us then, and went back to work on her grade book. It *was* a grade book she was working on. Standing close to her desk, I could see that she wasn't writing any notes to Pop.

But we did have a victory! Bailey and I hurried to the back of the room to discuss our plans. We drew up a list of the things we'd need: paper; an announcement for the intercom asking for news items; a box in the hall for people to drop in things they wanted to contribute; a typist or someone in the office to type up our stuff when we had it finished; the use of the mimeo machine. And about a thousand other things like pencils and crayons and drawing stuff.

By the time everybody else got there, Bailey and I had our plans all ready. Some of the kids were going to be really jealous that they hadn't thought of this first, especially when we got out of class for two hours a day. I couldn't believe that Bailey had really pulled that one off. She hadn't even asked *if* we could get time. Just—"How much?"

We did our morning exercises then, the Pledge, and the song. As usual, Bailey gave Miss Holt fits trying to figure out why it sounded all wrong. Instead of saying, "I pledge allegiance to the flag," Bailey had taught everyone to say, "I pitch a lizard to the flag." And although Holt frowned, you could see that she couldn't really tell what was wrong.

When everyone sat down, Miss Holt had Bailey and me come up to the front and tell everyone what we were planning to do. They were all surprised, and jealous, too, you could tell. Janie went into such a pout that I expected to see her begin sucking her thumb and rubbing her hair right there in class. Owen, who can't ever breathe with his mouth shut anyway, was panting like a dog and trying to get Miss Holt's attention: "Miss Huh . . . Miss Huh. . . ." But Miss Holt wouldn't look at him. Violet was bouncing her fat butt up and down off the chair waving her hand madly and trying to get Miss Holt's attention. But Holt just shook her head and didn't speak to any of them.

Finally, though, when Bailey and I were finished, and when it looked like Violet would break the chair or her rear end with bouncing, Miss Holt said, "Class, if you have suggestions or comments, speak to Bailey or Kevin. This is their project."

She went on a while longer, trying to quiet down the persistent ones like Violet, and while she talked, I watched her closely, trying to pretend I was Pop. Would Pop think she was pretty? If I were Pop, would I like her? It was so hard to tell. But Bailey was so sure. And anyway, we were a lot further along on our project than we were yesterday. And maybe today, Miss Holt would give me that note for Pop. A note with a big, fat *yes*.

15

THINGS WERE DEFINITELY getting out of control.

It was Tuesday afternoon, a week later, and we were in the coat closet, our things for the school paper spread out all over the place. There were pens and pencils and scissors and news items from the different classes, and glue and tape and big sheets of paper and little scraps of notes. And people. Lots of them. Not just Bailey and me. We had asked Miss Holt for help—all we wanted was Brant to help us go through some of the stuff that was dropped in the dump box in the hall. Holt had let us have Brant, but she insisted on getting some others to help us. She called them "fine writers." What they really were, were the weirdos of the world: Janie and Owen.

The paper wasn't all that was out of control. That morning, Miss Holt had finally—finally—after eight whole days, given me a note for Pop. Of course, as soon as recess time came, Bailey and I had snuck off to the side of the playground to open it and read it. Holt had agreed to "come for a visit sometime. Of course, Kevin would be present. Perhaps we could discuss his schoolwork or his plans for his future." She hadn't said anything at all about setting a date for dinner.

But Bailey was ecstatic, even while I was scared half to death.

"She'll come!" Bailey said. "She'll really do it! They'll talk about you for about two minutes, and then forget you because they'll fall in love. They won't be able to help it. It'll be perfect." She kept clenching her fists and doing that thumbs-up routine she loves to do.

"What makes you so sure they'll fall in love?" I asked. "And besides, now we have to write another note and ask for another definite date. And we can't do that until we're sure this newspaper is going to work out all right and we'll have enough money."

"You worry like an old woman!"

"Right. And you don't worry at all." I knew I was beginning to sound like a worrier, but if this didn't work out, it was my life, not hers, that was getting messed up. "Anyway," I said. "What makes you so sure they'll love each other?"

"She's pretty, right?" Bailey said.

"Yeah. For her age."

"And your father's a nice guy?"

"Yeah."

Bailey shrugged and turned away, as if she had settled it.

"It takes more than that, you know," I said. "There has to be something else . . . some—"

"What?"

"Chemistry," I said, because that's what people always say.

"What's that?"

"I'm not sure. I think it has something to do with sex.

You know . . . love. . . . Hmmm. Think I should write her some poems, some love stuff? Get her in the mood? I could slip them onto her desk, like they were from Pop—"

Bailey groaned. "And you were scared about writing another note asking for a date! What are you, nuts?"

She was right. Might as well leave it just the way it was.

The bell rang. Recess was over and it was time to go in.

And so now there we were, stuffed inside the coat closet—plenty of room for three, but so jammed with five of us that we couldn't work without touching each other. I kept pulling my arm away from Owen's because his was all wet and oily. And hairy. He has the hairiest arms I've ever seen. Everything about him is weird, including his name. He has more colds than anyone I've ever met. He talks and looks like his nose is always stuffed up, and his mouth just hangs there open all the time. His bottom lip is huge and juts out like the landing strip on an aircraft carrier. Bailey says it got that way from breathing through his mouth instead of his nose. But I don't believe her because his nose is huge, too. Besides, no matter what Holt says, he can't write worth a poop. So we didn't let him do any of the writing. Instead, we gave that to Brant, and we let Owen go through the stuff that had been dropped in the hall box that morning. The awful stuff he got to throw away, and the rest he had to give to us to decide if it was worth using.

And all the time, Bailey kept looking at me and whistling through her teeth, real softly, "Here Comes the Bride."

I reached across to where she was finishing a drawing of the school. It was huge, really good, too. She had filled in tiny details like the flagpole and the flowers outside, even kids walking up the school steps. Mrs. Tanner, the school secretary, said she'd reduce it in size and we'd use it for the front page of the paper. Bailey had been working on it for three days.

I bent close to the drawing, and with a Magic Marker, made swipes in the air real close to the paper.

"Hey, cut it out!" Bailey yelled. She yanked the paper to safety.

"Then shut up," I said.

Janie and Owen looked from me to Bailey and then back, with an expectant look on their faces that only wimpy kids get, the tell-me-what's-going-on look.

Brant kept right on writing.

I stared down the wimps till they looked away.

Bailey gave me her best innocent face, the one she uses on teachers. But she stopped whistling that song. She put aside the drawing and went back to working on her column, *News of the School*.

For a while, we all worked quietly. The only sound in the coat closet was Owen breathing.

"Look." Owen had a paper in his hand and was breathing over it. "Id's frob duh sickt-grade gul," he breathed.

"It's from a sixth-grade girl," Brant translated without looking up.

"I talk English!" Owen glared at him.

"Just joking," Brant said, and he smiled that smile that makes teachers fall in love with him. "What is it?" he continued, obviously trying to make up.

"A pome."

"A poem?" I reached over and snatched it out of his hand.

I had put one of my poems in the pile of things ready to go into the newspaper. Somehow in all the mess, it must have gotten into his pile.

The others were looking at me, but I just shrugged. "I'm the editor," I said, and I began studying the poem as if I'd never seen it before.

"Id's nod bad," Owen murmured.

Maybe he wasn't as dumb as he looked. Then I remembered he'd said it was from a girl so I made a face at him. I put the poem aside as though I were going to work on it later.

Bailey grinned at me over everyone's heads, but she didn't say anything.

After a bit, Bailey sighed. "God, it's boring to be a kid," she said, and she waved the sheet of paper she was writing on—the news of the school. Because she knew Miss Holt was going to be looking over what she'd written, she wasn't including any of her blackmail stuff and was just doing regular news.

"Listen to this," she said. "The first grade is doing a grandparents' day—'Lunch with your grandparents!' For Pete's sake, you can have lunch with your gramps any day."

"Nunh, uh!" Owen breathed.

He's the only person I know who says, "Nunh, uh," instead of "Uh-uh."

"*I* can't," Janie said, sounding even prissier than usual.

Bailey squinted at Janie, and I could just see she was

about to dare her—"How come?" or something like that. Then, as if she was reading Janie's mind, she said, "Well, it doesn't count if he's dead."

"Well, he is," Janie said, and she sounded proud of it.

"Doesn't count," Bailey said again. She read some more. "And listen to this. The second grade is having a dress-up day for Halloween. Why don't the *teachers* dress up or something? Old dragon-puss across the hall that Miss Holt hangs out with—she'd make a perfect witch. And then the stuck-up sixth graders are going to the Museum of Science and Industry. How's *that* for boring?"

Then her eyes caught mine, and she started to look funny. If she were in a cartoon, a light bulb would have come on over her head. "At night?" she whispered.

I knew what she was talking about. She's always thinking up new things to do, places to explore, like the top of the A & P. But a museum at *night*?

I looked quickly at Janie and then at Owen. Janie was writing away, her tongue caught between her teeth, a pencil stuffed behind one ear, making her hair stand out in a clump. Probably her idea of how to be a reporter. Owen was bent over his junk box, breathing like a diesel engine.

"Outside?" I whispered. "Or in?" I was thinking of books I'd read where kids get locked up in a museum at night. I wondered if she was thinking that, too.

"In." She grinned at me.

Behind us, the door opened, and Miss Holt stood there. She was wearing a red and white dress in a soft kind of material. Pop loves red. I hoped she'd wear it when she came to dinner.

Behind us, the door opened, and Miss Holt stood there.

"How's it going?" she asked.

"Very good, Miss Holt," Janie said.

"Who asked you?" Bailey said.

"Bailey." Miss Holt used her warning voice.

"Okay, okay," Bailey said. "Anyhow, it is going okay, but it's slow. It's going to take a lot more time."

"Then I'm afraid you'll have to do it after school hours," Miss Holt said.

For a minute, nobody spoke, except Bailey, who swore under her breath.

"Well, I did tell you a week, and it's been a week," Miss Holt said.

Janie blinked five quick times. I swear, she looked as if she was about to cry.

Owen didn't look up, but he snuffled like a wet seal. But then, Owen always snuffles.

Holt stood there for a second. "All right, all right," she said, probably because she was afraid Janie would weep all over the floor. "This is Tuesday. I'll give you till Friday. But if it takes longer, you'll have to do it after school. Is that fair?"

"Oh, yes, Miss Holt!" Janie and Owen said it together.

Brant just grunted.

I said, "Yes, Ma'am." If she was coming to dinner, I might as well begin to impress her.

Bailey sighed and rolled her eyes. "I guess," she said.

But when Miss Holt left, Bailey was grinning again. "Maybe on the weekend we'll try that," she said, and I knew she was talking about the museum.

"Try what?" Janie said.

Bailey stuck her face close to Janie's. "What are you talking about?"

"You're going to try something?" Janie said, sounding confused.

"Not trying anything."

Janie looked at me. "Didn't she just say. . . ."

I shrugged.

At the moment, sneaking into a museum didn't matter. What mattered was that we had to finish the school paper so we could sell it so we could make money for a dinner. Dinner for Pop and Miss Holt. That's what this was all about. And the paper was well on its way to being finished. Even though I was half scared to death by what we were actually planning to do, I was beginning to believe we could pull it off. Because at least the first part of the project had succeeded: Holt had agreed to come see Pop . . . sometime. Now it was just up to Bailey and me to make sure that the time was soon.

16

THE PAPER WAS finished. It had taken another whole week, and Bailey and I had spent hours after school for four days to do it. But now that it was done, it looked really professional. Miss Holt had approved it, and Mrs. Tanner, the school secretary, had typed it up and copied it. All Bailey and I had to do now was staple the pages together. We had well over three hundred copies made—enough for kids and teachers and extras in case anybody's parents wanted some. Even if we only sold three hundred at ten cents each, we'd have plenty for a great turkey dinner.

And we were going to need it, because in my pocket, at that moment, was another note from Miss Holt to Pop agreeing to come to dinner on the Saturday of Thanksgiving weekend. That was because the week before, Bailey and I had come up with another message, even more dignified and simple than the last. It said only, "Would Saturday, the 24th, at 6:00 P.M. do nicely?" The "nicely" part was Bailey's idea.

Holt's letter, which Bailey and I had read the moment we could get some privacy, said that she'd be pleased—although again, she wrote that it would be "with Kevin, of course."

So Bailey and I were in the little room off the school office after school on Friday, stapling papers together. Clump-clank. Clump-clank. We punched the stapler over and over.

"Three hundred papers is a he—heck of a lot of papers," I said. I examined the palm of my hand. It was red, and getting swollen right by my thumb.

"Money in the bank," Bailey muttered, even though she knew very well none of this money would ever see a bank. Her head was bent and her hair, as usual, was swinging in her eyes.

"Think we'll sell all of these?" I asked.

"Yup. We got news from all the classes. Everyone will buy it because people love to read about themselves."

"How's it going, children?" Mrs. Tanner's voice penetrated the little room like a voice from God on a TV show. But no TV show had God having a sing-songy voice like Mrs. Tanner's.

Bailey shook her hair out of her eyes. "Oh, it's fine, Mrs. Tanner," she sang back, in the same kind of sing-songy voice. She grinned at me.

"That's go . . . oood," Mrs. Tanner called.

I grinned. Mrs. Tanner didn't even seem to notice that Bailey was making fun of her.

"Are you almost finished?" she called again. "I'm ready to go ho . . . oome!"

"Then, go . . . ooo!" I called back, but real softly, not loud enough for her to hear.

We shuffled through papers, trying to figure out how many we still had to do. A third? A quarter, maybe?

Mrs. Tanner put her head around the doorway and beamed in on us. Her face is round and moon-like, and all her features are small and sort of squashed flat against her face like an elephant had stepped on it. Her body's all round and mushy-looking, too.

"How much longer?" she asked.

"Not much," I said. "We've done a lot." I pointed to the pile of finished newspapers beside us.

She fluttered her little, piggy eyelids. "Ooooh, your class is going to have so much money in their treasury."

"*What?*" Bailey and I said it together.

"In the treasury," she repeated. "Miss Holt says maybe you'll all take a trip to the museum."

The phone rang in the outer office, and she ducked her head out of the doorway and disappeared.

Bailey and I stared at each other.

"No way," I said.

"Never," Bailey said.

"I'll burn them first," I said.

"I'll help you," Bailey answered.

And then we both just looked at each other.

In a moment, Miss Tanner was back. Miss Holt was with her.

"How's it going?" Mrs. Tanner asked, as if she hadn't just said that about two seconds ago. A programmed robot.

Miss Holt picked up one of the finished, stapled papers and flipped through it. "You've done a really professional job." She sounded surprised.

"*We* did it," I said.

"Of course you did," Miss Holt answered.

"The money's ours!" Bailey blurted.

Miss Holt looked surprised but she didn't say anything.

"It's ours!" Bailey said again, swinging her head hard so her hair was out of her eyes. When I looked at her, I was startled because her eyes were super-bright as if she were about to cry. "We worked for it. It's ours!" She bent and began punching the stapler fiercely, her hair falling back over her face again, so I couldn't see her eyes anymore. *Was* she crying?

"It was a class project," Miss Holt said quietly.

"Nuts to that!" Bailey shot back. But her voice came out as if she was squeezing it past something in her throat, just like the day we'd done the letter-writing in class. I recognized that sound.

I looked at Holt, expecting her to get mad at Bailey, but I could tell by the look on her face that she had heard the sound in Bailey's voice, too.

"But others helped," Miss Holt said calmly. "What about Janie and Owen and Brant?"

"We did ninety percent of the work," Bailey answered, and still she didn't look up. She continued mashing the stapler down on the pages. "We did it. We thought it up. It was our project. *Ours.*"

Holt opened her mouth, then closed it again. She looked at me, an odd look as if I could give her some help.

There was a long silence.

I bent and began stapling pages again, too. Miss Holt just stood there silently. Mrs. Tanner popped out of the room as the phone rang again.

"How about you keep some and the rest goes to the class treasury?" Holt asked.

"No," Bailey said.

"Maybe," I said at the same time.

Miss Holt sighed, and I got a weird feeling—I felt sorry for her. It was as if she wanted to do what we wanted, but she felt she shouldn't, too.

I decided to help her.

"How about we share with Janie and Owen and Brant?" I asked. "That would be fair, wouldn't it?"

I half-expected Bailey to shout "no!" but she didn't say a word. She only punched harder on the stapler. Her hand was going to be really sore.

Miss Holt kept looking at Bailey's bent head. She watched her for a very, very long time. And then she said, "I think that would be fair." But she kept standing there.

Mrs. Tanner's mushed face appeared in the doorway again. "How's it going?" she asked again. For the third time.

Reprogram the robot, I begged silently.

"Shut up," Bailey said softly, but I heard her.

I looked quickly at Miss Holt and Mrs. Tanner, but if Holt heard, she didn't show it.

"Just fine," Miss Holt said. She went to the door, and I saw her put a hand against Mrs. Tanner's wide body, and sort of push her backward out of the door.

The two of them disappeared into the main office, leaving Bailey and me alone.

"Well," Bailey said after a minute. "We don't have that much time left." She sounded as if she were defending herself. "How were we going to get money if this didn't work? Even if we thought up something else, we'd never get it done fast enough."

"I know." I wasn't arguing with her, though she sounded like I was. I had a feeling that something else was on her mind.

"It's gotta work," Bailey said. "If it doesn't, in two weeks you'll be gone. You'll be *history*." There was that choked sound in her voice again, and she mashed the stapler so hard that the spring popped out.

Together, we fixed the stapler. Neither of us said anything more while we finished putting together the rest of the papers. It took only about twenty minutes, and then we cleaned up the place. When we left, the papers were neatly stacked, all ready for sale on Monday morning.

17

NINETEEN DOLLARS and thirty cents. All of it in nickels, dimes, and pennies. Mostly pennies.

By the following Friday, that's all we had collected. That was it. And the dinner party was the next night.

We had done everything to sell papers, everything we could think of. We sold them before school, after school, and in the cafeteria at lunchtime. When we got desperate, we sold them outside school to people on the street, even though Miss Holt told us not to. Actually, that's where we made most of our money, and some people even paid us more for the papers than we asked. One man gave us a whole dollar. I think people were just curious to see what a school paper was like and what was going on in a school. Maybe some of them felt sorry for us, the way you do for little kids selling drinks at a lemonade stand. Bailey and I didn't care, though. We needed money. We'd take money any way we could get it.

The only real problem we'd had so far was Janie. She almost had a seizure when she found out that Bailey and I were getting to keep the money and only giving her what we decided was fair. Bailey had decided that fair was a dollar. I thought it was more like two dollars or maybe even three, but that only lasted until Friday when I found out that we had just nineteen dollars. Then I agreed with Bailey that one dollar was plenty. Even then, it almost made me choke to hand a dollar to Janie and to Owen. Brant got two dollars. Bailey and I agreed on that, and Brant promised not to tell the others how much he got.

And so, on Saturday morning, Bailey and I were standing in front of the A & P, waiting when it opened. The money—now, after paying off Brant and Janie and Owen, down to $15.30—was weighing down the pockets of our jeans and jackets, even though we had put the pennies inside an old zippered case that used to hold a tennis racket.

This was the day. The dinner we had planned so carefully. Miss Holt was coming, and Pop still didn't know. It was going to be the best dinner anyone had ever made. We could only pray that they'd fall in love. They had to. It was our last chance.

As soon as the store opened, we rushed in and grabbed a cart. The first thing we did was to clunk the zippered case into the cart. It must have weighed as much as Mrs. Tanner.

Bailey pushed the cart, while I read the list and checked off prices. We had pushed the tiny turkey way to the back of the case when we'd first priced things weeks ago, and we looked for it right away. It was hard to tell which one was ours, because there were lots of small turkeys now.

"This is weird," I said to Bailey. "There's a million little turkeys here now. And Bailey, they're cheap! Lookit this one. It's only nine dollars."

"Grab it," Bailey said. "Quick! Maybe they mispriced it and they'll change their minds."

We both bent into the case of frozen turkeys. We could see our breath in there it was so icy. There was no doubt—you could get turkeys a lot cheaper now than last month. We rummaged through them, looking for the smallest one, but the best we could do was the nine dollar job. Our hands were frozen by the time we got through.

"Okay," Bailey said. "Mark it down. Nine dollars and three cents for the turkey."

I wrote it down.

We aimed our cart for the aisle with the cranberry sauce, canned sweet potatoes, and canned gravy. We zinged one can of each into the cart, added it up, and decided we could afford more. We retraced the aisle and added an extra can of each and a can of olives, too. Black olives. Pop loves them, and olives look good on a Thanksgiving table.

Two dollars and twenty-nine cents left.

We headed for the aisle with the cake mix and icing mix. Icing mix is expensive! But by going through the different brands, we came up with a can of it we could afford. With thirteen cents left over.

We were up in the front, starting for the checkout, when Bailey said, "Halt!"

"Huh?"

"Gotta look 'em over." She was nodding toward the people manning the checkout stations.

"Why?"

"Because they're going to blow their guts when we give them fifteen dollars in mostly pennies. We have to pick the right one."

I looked them over pretty carefully, but I couldn't tell by looking which one was apt to blow his or her guts. I figured that the lady with the gray frizzy hair and half glasses and needle-shaped nose was out. Anyone who looked like that would have to feel mean.

There was a fat bald man with a few hairs brushed from one ear straight across the top of his head to the other ear. He had kind of a friendly look. And a fat woman who kind of reminded me of Mrs. Tanner with her moon face.

Bailey saw that I was looking at the moon-faced one, and she nodded. "Yup. That's the one. Motherly. Now watch this."

She headed for the fat woman's checkout and began unloading the stuff. The woman's name was Arlene. It said so on a black plastic badge that she wore on her front.

"I hope you don't mind if we give you some change," Bailey said, and she sounded little-girl-like, timid, in a way I'd never heard before.

I knew I was going to have trouble not laughing through this one.

"Can always use some change," Arlene said.

"We've saved up our allowance," Bailey said.

Arlene's eyebrows went up. "For dinner?"

"A special dinner. Our father's birthday," Bailey said. And she still used that little-girl voice.

"Aah," Arlene said. "That's sweet." She smiled at Bailey.

I thought I'd choke.

When everything had been rung up but not totaled, Arlene said, "Any coupons?"

Bailey and I looked at each other. We'd never even thought of coupons.

"No," I said.

"There are some in the front of the store," Arlene said.

I just looked at her blankly. I thought you had to bring your own coupons with you, like from the newspaper or something.

"Come here." She stepped away from the register and around to the front of her little booth, beckoning us to follow her.

Up by the front of the store, on a little metal stand, were some store flyers with printed coupons on them. Arlene picked up a flyer, tore out a coupon, and handed it to me: "Seventy-five cents off any turkey, eight pounds or more."

Bailey looked at it. "Thanks!" she said. She forgot to use her little-girl voice, but Arlene didn't seem to notice.

Back at the register, Arlene totaled it all up and then, while Bailey and I watched—had we added right?—she subtracted one dollar and fifty cents. "Double coupons," she said. It came to $13.67.

"Wait!" Bailey raced off to the back of the store, leaving me to begin counting out the pennies.

I didn't dare look at Arlene.

In about half a minute, Bailey was back, pushing her way past the people lined up behind us. She had two more items—a bag of chips and a little metal can of dip stuff. She plopped them down on the counter. "Hors d'oeuvres," she panted. And she gave Arlene her little-girl smile.

Either it worked, or else Arlene was one of those saint kind of people that they tell you about in Bible class, because she didn't get upset or annoyed or anything. It must have taken fifteen minutes to count out everything and make sure it was right, and she didn't complain once. But the man right behind us in the aisle kept muttering, "Why me? I don't believe this. Why me?"

When it was all totaled up, we had exactly six cents left. When Arlene handed it to us, she said, "Have a nice dinner. And tell him 'happy birthday' for me."

On our way out of the store, Bailey and I stopped to use our six cents in the gum machine. There was a little kid standing there staring into the little glass bubble thing. Bailey just stuck the change in his hand.

At home, we spread all the stuff out on the kitchen table. Pop was working the way he does most Saturdays, so we had the house and the kitchen completely to ourselves. He knew we were planning a surprise for him that night, and even though he'd kept saying, "Don't do anything fancy," I could tell that he was pleased. He thought it was for his birthday. He had no idea what kind of fancy birthday present we were planning.

As we unpacked the stuff, I said to Bailey, "Are you getting nervous?"

"About cooking a turkey?"

"No. About what we're going to be doing tonight."

"Nah. Are you?"

"Yeah. I keep picturing Holt walking up that sidewalk and Pop here in the kitchen or the living room, not even knowing what's about to happen."

Bailey sucked on her hair for a while. "Maybe we ought to tell him. But not till the last minute, right before she gets here. That way he can't back out."

"If only he wasn't so shy!" We'd been over and over this, and always Bailey reassured me, and always I wanted

124

to believe her. But now that the day was actually here, I was pretty nervous. Not only that Pop would get upset. But what if the whole scheme didn't work? We'd be leaving on Monday. Actually *leaving*! Anything we were taking was already packed up.

Bailey thumped the turkey hard on its chest, the way a doctor thumps you when you're having a checkup. She said, "He's lonely—not the turkey, your father. She's available. And it's all going to work out great."

"And if it doesn't, this is my last weekend here."

"Trust me," Bailey said. She frowned at the directions on the turkey bag. "Twenty minutes to the pound. This sucker weighs nine pounds. So that's . . . a hundred and eighty minutes, right?"

"Right," I said. "Three hours."

I tried squeezing the turkey. It was as hard as the ice on a lake in midwinter. If you dropped it on your foot, you'd break your toes off. "You sure it'll be done in three hours?" I said.

Bailey shrugged, and read the directions again. "That's what the chart says."

I looked, too. She was right. Twenty minutes to the pound.

So we put the turkey in the freezer part of the refrigerator, pushing aside ice cream and frozen pizza, until it was time to put it in the oven. That would be three o'clock if Holt was coming at six.

Then Bailey and I got out a pad of paper and a pencil and started making a list. We started at six-thirty, and worked all the way back to noon. It went something like this:

6:30 Lovers sit down to dinner.

6:15 Serve hors d'oeuvres in the living room.

6:00 Miss Holt arrives. Greeted by Pop.

5:45 Arrange hors d'oeuvres in dish; ice cake.

5:30 Sweet potatoes go in oven.

5:15 Cake goes in oven.

5:00 Prepare cake mix.

4:45 Open canned potatoes; open canned gravy; put in pots on stove. Open cranberry sauce. Put in refrigerator.

It was a long list, and it even included things like cleaning the bathroom and vacuuming. Because it was all written out, we knew we weren't going to forget one thing. And that was really important, because we wanted it to be really special. It was going to be a night we'd remember.

18

WE WERE READY.

The house was cleaned. The turkey was cooking, and the turkey smell was everywhere in the house. Sweet potatoes were in a dish on top of the stove, waiting to go in the oven. The gravy was opened and in a pan on top of the stove. The cranberries were in the best dish I could find in the house—a milky white one with edges that were shaped like petals on flowers. The olives were in a matching dish that was just a little smaller. The cake was in the oven, ready to come out any minute. The table was set, and we had even picked some fall flowers that were still blooming at the edge of the yard. Actually, they were in the yard next door, but it was so close that it could have been our yard. We had put the flowers in the center of the table.

Pop was in the shower getting ready.

And my stomach was doing the meanest things it had done since I ate the goldfish.

Bailey, even though she didn't say so, was getting a little nervous, too. She got awfully quiet, and even looked a little pale.

I was opening the chips and putting them in a basket with a napkin under them when Pop came into the kitchen. His hair was still wet from the shower, and he smelled of after-shave lotion. He had that fresh-washed look that I like so much, and even though I was nervous, I couldn't help smiling at him.

He smiled back. "What's this *two* places set at the table?" he asked. "Bailey's eating with us." He turned to her. "You are, aren't you?"

Bailey looked at me.

Me at her.

Now was the time to tell him, wasn't it?

"Uh . . . no," Bailey said.

"No?" Pop looked so disappointed.

"Uh, no," Bailey said again. "Can't."

"I'm sorry. Well . . ." Pop grinned at me. "Then I guess it's just you and me, huh?"

"Uh, no. Not exactly."

I poked Bailey.

She poked me back.

I poked her again. This was her idea. She should tell him.

"What is this?" Pop was laughing. "You two going to make me eat alone? And on my birthday?"

"No," I said. "Not alone." I swallowed hard. "You're having a guest. A surprise guest."

Pop tilted his head and his eyebrows went up. He stopped laughing. "Oh?" he said.

His not laughing made me even more nervous. "Yeah." I finished dumping the chips into the basket.

"Who?" Pop said, very quietly.

I looked at Bailey. The least she could do was say

something. This was all her idea. She was standing there like somebody's puppet or dummy or something.

"Miss Holt," she said. Her voice came out squeaky.

"Miss *who?*"

"Miss Holt." This time she didn't squeak. But she took the basket from me and began rearranging the chips.

I took it back from her.

Pop took the basket from both of us. "Look at me," he said. "Who. Is. Coming. To. Dinner?" Each word clipped off like it was a separate sentence.

I looked at Bailey. She looked at me. Together, we said, "Miss Holt?" But it came out like we'd said it with a question mark.

"Who is Miss Holt?"

"You know," I said. "Miss Holt . . . my teacher."

"Your teacher?" Pop couldn't have sounded more surprised if I had told him that Benjamin Franklin was coming to dinner. "Why?"

"We invited her."

"*You* invited her. Actually," Bailey said.

Pop sat down at the kitchen table. "I think you'd better explain."

Bailey looked at me, and then she began to talk, that real firm, grown-up way that she does sometimes. "It's your birthday so we wanted to surprise you. So we invited Miss Holt to your birthday dinner." She went and opened the oven door and peeked in, poking the turkey a little, as though she'd been doing a turkey dinner every day since she was six. "Almost done." She smiled at me.

"Bailey." From his voice, I could tell that Pop wasn't about to be distracted by a turkey cooking. "Bailey, you said before that *I* invited her."

"You did. Sort of." She was smiling, but at the look on Pop's face, her face got tight and the smile sort of seeped away. "Okay, Mr. Corbett, it's this way. We sent a note to Miss Holt, asking her to come here to dinner. . . ." She paused.

"Yes?"

"And we pretended it was from you." She blurted it out real fast.

She looked at me.

Pop looked at me.

I nodded. "Right," I said.

"*Right*?" Pop's face got blazing red, like he'd just gotten a sunburn. It went right up into his hair and into that little part above his forehead that was getting bald. "You signed my name to something, and didn't tell me about it?" His voice was quivering and he stood up and looked around the kitchen like he thought we were totally mad-crazy or something. "I don't believe you'd do a thing like that, Kevin!" He had a look on his face that I'd never seen before, and I suddenly realized what it was. He was mad. Really mad.

Nobody spoke for a moment. Then Pop said, "Okay. But you two are going to have to handle this. I'm leaving."

"*What*?" I said.

"Wait!" Bailey said.

"I'm sorry." Pop shook his head, and left the kitchen. "But wait. . . ."

Pop was already halfway across the dining room and he stopped, but he didn't turn around.

I don't know how long I stood there trying to figure out just the right words to say. Something. Something had to make him change his mind. But all I could think of to say was "What about the dinner?"

"What about it?" Pop said quietly, still without turning around.

What about it? "It's a turkey" was all I could think of.

For a long minute, Pop just stood there, and then he sighed and turned around and came back to the kitchen. He stood in the doorway for the longest time, and then he said, "This has just got to be the weirdest moment in my life."

Both Bailey and I knew enough not to say a word.

We waited. And waited.

Finally, Pop groaned and pushed his hands through his hair. He shook his head at me. "You and me? We're going to have to have a talk. Afterwards."

"That mean you'll stay?"

"I'll stay."

"Thanks," I said.

"O-kay!" Bailey whispered.

Pop looked at me again as if he were about to say something more. But then he left the kitchen and went into the living room.

Neither Bailey nor I said another word. We just stood there, looking at the clock. I don't know what Bailey was thinking, but I was praying that the clock would stop and six o'clock would never get there.

19

ONE SECOND. Two seconds. Four. Six. Eight.

How much longer before Pop answered the door? Or wasn't he going to answer it at all?

Bailey and I were hiding out in the kitchen, neither of us even daring to peek out. The doorbell had rung, but Pop wasn't answering it. Had he changed his mind and left?

The bell rang again. I was just about to give up and answer it myself, when I heard Pop open the door. And then I did something that I haven't done since I was about four years old—I stuck my fingers hard into my ears and began humming. Humming, humming, humming. So I couldn't hear what was being said in the hall.

At first, Bailey stared at me like I had just lost a big piece of my mind. But in an instant, she was doing the same thing.

After a minute, I moved my fingers. Nothing. No sound at all. They weren't even speaking!

Oh, hell.

Bailey was listening, too, her fingers poised just outside her ears so she could stick them right back in in a hurry if she needed to.

"They hate each other," I said.

"Maybe they're kissing," Bailey said.

"Sure," I said.

The buzzer on the stove rang, and Bailey and I both jumped for it. Time to take out the cake.

I grabbed for the pot holders, and almost knocked over Bailey who was reaching for them, too.

"I'll do it," I said.

"No, me," Bailey said.

"Me."

"*Me.*"

We were both frantic to do *something* besides listen to the silence. "We'll do it together," I said.

Bailey took out one pan and I took out the other. They looked pretty good, but when I stuck in a toothpick, it came out wet. They were still not done in the middle.

"No good," I said. I reset the timer for five minutes. "They have to go back in."

"I'll do it," Bailey said. "You bring the hors d'oeuvres in to them."

"Forget that! *You* bring in the hors d'oeuvres."

"Scared?" she said.

"Yeah, I'm scared. You?"

"A little." She put the cake pan back in the oven. "A lot," she added.

Both of us were quiet for a while, listening to the voices from the living room. Actually, there weren't any voices. They must have been just sitting there staring at each other or out the window.

Bailey straightened up, putting her shoulders back. "We'll bring in the stuff together. You bring the basket. I'll bring the dip."

"Okay." I nodded and picked up the basket. Bailey picked up the dip.

We stopped at the kitchen door.

Stared at each other.

And then we both went into the living room.

Pop was seated at one end of the couch, and Miss Holt was on the edge of a chair across the room from him. She had chosen the little chair that has threads peeling off the arms, and springs that poke at your bottom. She had this kind of wild look in her eyes.

A mouse—out from under the grandfather clock—about to run and hide from the vacuum. That's just what she looked like.

"Kevin! Bailey!" Miss Holt sounded like a mother who had just found her long-lost children.

"Hi," I said.

"Hi," Bailey said.

"Well!" Pop said.

We put the chips and dip down on the table between them. Miss Holt's chair was so far away that she couldn't possibly reach the table except by stretching so far out of her chair she'd surely fall off.

"Sit down! Sit down!" Miss Holt was frantically patting the arm of her chair.

Sit on the arm of her chair? Grown-ups were bizarre.

"Yes, do. Please do!" Pop was patting the sofa beside him.

I looked at Bailey. Now it was her who got the mouse look.

Pop was seated at one end of the couch, and Miss Holt was on the edge of a chair across the room from him.

"We can't," I said. "We're working."

"Oh, but you have to!" Miss Holt said.

The buzzer sounded in the kitchen, and Bailey and I both took off like it was a shot for the start of a race. We almost tripped over each other getting to the kitchen.

We closed the door behind us, and I leaned back against it.

Bailey went and turned off the buzzer.

"Oh, God!" I said. "This is so awful. Just pray that Pop doesn't tell her we did this. If she finds out, we're—"

"Dead," Bailey finished for me. "Or expelled. We end our school career now, in fifth grade." She scratched her head. "Actually," she said, "that wouldn't be such a bad thing."

We were quiet again, listening. Still no sound coming from the living room.

We took the cakes out of the oven and tested them. This time they were done.

Bailey tore open the can of frosting. She did it fiercely, like she was ripping the top off someone's head. "Look," she said. "The heck with them. We're doing the best we can. This is one real good dinner, and if they don't like it—tough."

"Yeah." I nodded. "Right. We've spent a lot of time and all this money, and we went through the whole thing with the paper and all. If they don't like it—tough."

"Right," Bailey said. "Besides, as soon as they have dinner, it'll be better. They'll have something to talk about."

"Yeah," I agreed. "It's always hard when you first meet someone, to find something to say."

We each took one layer of the cake and a knife, and began spreading frosting on the layers.

After a minute, I asked, "Is your icing disappearing?"

"Yeah. Is yours?"

"Yeah. I think it's sinking in." I sighed. "Probably because we bought the cheapest kind."

"I don't know." Bailey was reading the printing on the side of the can. "Uh-oh. It says here to let the cake cool. You think that's what's wrong?"

"Who knows? Who cares?"

There was still no sound from the living room. I looked at the clock. Six-twenty. Ten minutes before the turkey was supposed to be done. Ten minutes wouldn't matter. Close enough. "Let's bring this stuff to the table," I said.

Together, Bailey and I brought everything into the small dining room. Anyone would have had to admit that it looked sensational. The turkey was golden-brown and crispy. Beside it lay the carving fork and knife for Pop. The cranberry sauce and olives in their matching glass dishes looked super. We had put brown sugar on top of the sweet potatoes and it was now all golden on top. Steam was coming up from the gravy in the gravy dish. It all looked like those pictures you see on holiday calendars— turkey dinner at Grandma's.

I nudged Bailey. "You call them."

"*You* call them."

"I asked you first."

"I'll choose you," she said. "Odds or evens?"

"Odds," I said.

"Once, twice, three . . . shoot!"

Odds.

Evens.

Odds.

Odds.

I won.

"Go. Do it," I said.

She marched off into the living room like she was about to be executed.

In a minute, Pop and Miss Holt, also looking like they were going to execution, marched into the dining room behind her.

"Will you join us?" Pop asked Bailey and me. But from the glum sound in his voice I knew that he knew that we wouldn't.

"Oh, yes, do! Please!" Miss Holt said. That crazy, wild look was still in her eyes.

"No!" Bailey and I both said it together.

"We have stuff to do in the kitchen," I added.

"But . . ." Miss Holt looked positively wild.

"For dessert! We'll join you for dessert!" Bailey said. She gave one of her dazzling smiles like she does sometimes with grown-ups.

I'm not sure it worked perfectly, but neither Pop nor Miss Holt said one more thing about it. They were resigned, you could tell.

Then, just as we were about to go back in the kitchen, I saw Pop do something, and I knew that things were going to get better. He came around the table and held the chair for Miss Holt.

Out in the kitchen, after we had closed the door, I said to Bailey, "You see that?"

"Yup." She knew instantly what I was talking about.

"It's going to be okay, you watch. As soon as they start to eat."

And we were right. Out there in the kitchen, we could suddenly hear laughter coming from the dining room. First Miss Holt, and then Pop, and then Miss Holt again. They were practically hysterical. They sounded like two little kids.

In between the laughter, we could hear them talking. We couldn't hear what they were saying, and we didn't try. It didn't matter. They were talking, talking, talking. And then they'd laugh some more, and then they'd talk some more.

I nudged Bailey, and together we tiptoed to the door, and inched it open just a crack. I put my face to the crack, but all I could see was the edge of the dining room table. I didn't dare open the door any further, or they'd have noticed. But just then, Pop let out this terrific shout of laughter, and Holt laughed so hard that you could practically feel the floor shake.

I let the door close softly, and I turned to Bailey.

"Are they laughing too hard?" I said.

She shrugged.

Both of us sat down at the kitchen table and relaxed. It didn't matter how hard they were laughing. It was sure better than the silence.

20

AFTER A WHILE, their laughter quieted down, and we could just hear the soft hum of their voices. They must have found something to say, plenty to say, because they went on and on.

I stopped worrying completely. When things were awful, like before, you could tell. And you could also tell when they were going okay. This was definitely okay.

Bailey and I got the kitchen pretty much cleaned up, and then put on the water for instant coffee, and got out the cake plates. Although we had agreed to have dessert with them, we thought that by now they might not need us. Might not even want us.

At seven-thirty, we finally came out of the kitchen. We each carried a tray that we were going to use to carry away the dishes. That's because Bailey said it was sophisticated to do it that way, even though the only trays we had were kind of dented-up tin ones. Bailey also had a towel draped over her arm, which I thought was overdoing it.

Pop and Miss Holt were sitting across the table from

each other, and they had pushed their plates aside. They were still nibbling, though—olives. That had been a good choice to buy. They had eaten up practically every last olive, and the plate was covered with yucky, gnawed-on pits.

They both smiled at us when we came in—not those frozen smiles like before, but nice, old friendly smiles. Maybe Pop and I wouldn't have to have that "talk."

"Wonderful dinner," Miss Holt said. All her lipstick was worn away, and she looked so relaxed and ordinary, not at all the way she looked at school. That wild look was gone from her eyes. She could have been a teenager. I wondered just how old she really was.

"It was super," Pop agreed.

"Thank you," we both said.

Bailey and I began clearing the table of plates and serving dishes. Pop and Miss Holt had eaten up all the sweet potatoes, all the cranberries, and every olive. But there was an awful lot of turkey left. In fact, practically the entire turkey was there still.

I looked at their dinner plates. No turkey scraps at all.

"You didn't eat the turkey," I said.

Miss Holt looked at Pop. "Uh . . . no."

"Why?" I said.

"How come?" Bailey said at the same time.

"Uh . . ." Pop hesitated, and didn't look at me. "It's . . . uh . . . it's frozen . . . sort of."

"Frozen?" I said.

"Three-fifty degrees, twenty minutes to the pound," Bailey said. "Nine pounds, that's three hours." The look on her face dared them to disagree with her.

"Did you defrost it first?" Miss Holt asked.

"What's that mean? You mean, like let it melt?" Bailey asked.

Miss Holt nodded. "Yes, uh, like let it melt."

"Why would we do that?" Bailey asked.

Pop and Miss Holt both burst out laughing at the same time. Pop laughed so hard that tears came to his eyes. Then he must have seen the looks on our faces, because he reached his arm out to me and pulled me close to him.

"I'm sorry, son," he said. But from his face, I could tell that he was still trying awfully hard not to laugh. "This is why."

He pulled the turkey platter close to him, and reached inside the turkey. He felt around some, then took his hand out and said, "You do it."

I did. It was pretty cool inside.

"It's still frozen?" I said.

Pop nodded. "Kind of." He reached inside the turkey again and pulled something out. It looked like a little bag of some sort. Is that how turkeys were made inside?

But no, there was writing on the bag.

"What is it?" I said.

"Giblets and liver and stuff. You're supposed to defrost the turkey. And then you take this stuff out."

"Oh."

Pop still had his arm around my waist, and he hugged me to him. "Hey, don't worry about it," he said. "It was a very good dinner."

I pulled away. I didn't want him hugging me in front of Holt. "Yeah, without the turkey," I said. I couldn't believe how bad I felt.

"We ate some of it," Miss Holt said. "We did! Look,

the outside part was just fine, so we had a couple of slices. Really."

I looked from her to Pop to Bailey.

Bailey just shrugged. It didn't seem to bother her much.

"I know dessert will be wonderful," Miss Holt said.

How'd she know?

"But you must join us," Holt said. "You promised."

Bailey gave me that raised eyebrow look. Yes? No? We both knew we didn't want to interfere with them if they were falling in love.

"A deal's a deal," Pop said.

When he said that, I knew I didn't have much choice. Pop and I have that kind of understanding. "Okay," I said.

Bailey and I made a couple of trips from the dining room to the kitchen, bringing out the plates and leftovers and serving dishes and bringing in the dessert. Every time we closed the kitchen door behind us, Bailey began doing this little dance step, and sort of strutting, with her thumbs up, singing, "We did it, we did it, we did it, we *did* it!"

We brought in the coffee, then got the cake. The cake looked a little strange, like it didn't have any icing at all because it had all seeped in. But we had already broken off little pieces and it tasted fine.

We came in and sat down with Pop and Miss Holt.

Pop had never looked happier and Miss Holt had never looked so relaxed. We had done the right thing. I knew now that Pop wouldn't be mad at me. The only thing he'd feel bad about was that he hadn't thought of this himself. And that's why he'd never admit to Holt that this wasn't all his doing.

Bailey looked so pleased with herself, that I could just imagine her still humming, *We did it, we did it,* inside her head. The grin on her face reminded me of the Cheshire Cat—such a big smile that even after the cat had gone, the smile remained. I had the feeling that every time I walked into this room for the next week, I'd see her smile, still there above her chair.

And I *would* be walking into this room next week. I knew it. I wouldn't be getting in Pop's new car and driving to Oklahoma. All you had to do was take one look at Pop's face to know.

"This cake is delicious," Miss Holt said. "Where did you get this recipe for the glaze on top? It's so good."

"My grandmother's recipe," Bailey said, with an absolutely straight face.

Does your grandmother always put icing on hot cakes? I thought. Bailey and I exchanged looks, but neither of us even cracked a smile.

"You two are to be congratulated," Miss Holt went on. "You've done a really fantastic job."

"You sure have," Pop said.

Bailey and I just smiled.

"How did you learn to cook so good?" Pop said. "And money . . . you must have been saving your allowance for a long time, huh?"

He didn't really look as if he expected an answer and I wasn't sure, especially with Holt there, that I wanted to explain.

I looked at Bailey, and then quickly at Miss Holt. Holt was staring down into her plate.

There was quiet for a while as we all finished our cake.

"There's something I want to know," Pop said. "We want to know."

We?

I saw Pop glance across the table at Miss Holt. A silent question, I could see it in his face, and she nodded like she was answering him.

"We want to know whose idea this was," Pop said. He looked first at me, then at Bailey.

Silence.

"Was it yours, Kevin?" And when I didn't answer him he turned to Bailey. "Or was it yours?"

"Like—like to make you dinner?" Bailey said. She tried to look away from him but couldn't. Pop can lock eyes even better than Bailey when he wants to. "Uh . . . it was both our ideas." She smiled then. "For your birthday."

"I didn't mean the supper part," Pop said.

I tried to say, "What then?" but the words got stuck inside and I couldn't even move my lips.

Bailey's head came up and her eyes met mine. *Play dumb. We haven't any idea what he's talking about.* If she had written it out I couldn't have seen more clearly the message she was sending me.

Pop smiled a little. "No sense trying to fake it," he said. "We know."

Miss Holt nodded.

"Know what?" Bailey said. She tried to sound tough, but she ended up sounding a little sick.

Miss Holt spoke. "That one of you . . . or both of you . . . masterminded a plot to invite me here."

I felt sicker than Bailey had sounded. Sick, sick, sick. He knew. She knew. Pop had told. . . .

146

"Don't look like that," Pop said to me. "It's okay. In fact, you're pretty smart."

"Oh, good!" Bailey said.

But she shouldn't have spoken because Pop locked eyes with her again. "We just want to know why," he said.

"Why?" she said.

"Why."

"Oh."

Nobody said anything.

Pop was holding onto Bailey's eyes like she was a fish on the end of a string. It wasn't me he was doing that to, so he must have known I wouldn't tell him. So he probably had an idea why.

Bailey bent her head and examined her little chewed-up fingernails. She shrugged. "Because. Why not?"

Nobody spoke.

We couldn't tell! A question went between me and Bailey, a silent one, just like the look Pop and Miss Holt had exchanged before. *Should we tell*? she was saying. *No*, I answered. But they weren't going to let us go without some answer, so I decided to tell them half the story. That we wanted Pop to have a friend, and we chose someone—Miss Holt.

I took a deep breath. "Because," I said. "We thought that maybe you needed a friend. And if you met Miss Holt—" I stopped. I was dying of embarrassment. How could Pop make me say this in front of Holt?

"That if you guys met," Bailey interrupted, real matter-of-factly. "That if you guys met, maybe you'd like each other. Maybe even fall in love."

Pop laughed right out loud. Miss Holt did, too. Bailey laughed, too, but not quite as hard. I wasn't sure whether to laugh or not.

"So why'd you want me to be in love so bad?" Pop said, when he'd finished laughing.

And *that* was one we weren't going to answer.

"So you wouldn't move!" Bailey said immediately.

"Bailey!" I said. I didn't believe she'd said that.

There couldn't have been a worse silence in the room if someone had dropped dead on the table. Or thrown up all over the cake. It went on for a very long time.

"All this?" Pop said finally. He spoke so softly that I could barely hear him and he made a weird kind of gesture, sort of sweeping his hand around the room, toward the table, us sitting there. "All this . . . so we wouldn't move?"

He turned to me and his face was pale, sort of the way it had been in the kitchen before, right before he got mad and turned red. I couldn't tell if he was about to get mad again or something else. He didn't say anything else, just stared at me.

Silence. It went on and on and on. Even Bailey didn't break it with one of her dumb comments. She just chewed silently on her fingernails and I prayed for the phone to ring or lightning to hit the house or something.

"Well," Miss Holt said, after six days of silence went by. "I guess it's time for me to go." She pushed her chair back from the table.

Nobody argued with her.

"Can I take you home on my way?" she said to Bailey.

"No," Bailey said. "I have to help Kevin clean up here."

"I'll help him," Pop said. "You go."

He didn't sound as if we should argue with him.

I stood up and Bailey stood up, and Pop and Miss Holt stood up, and then all four of us walked to the door and said good-night like four well-trained robots. Mrs. Tanner would have been proud of us. I dreaded the moment alone with Pop when the door closed behind the other two.

But the only thing that happened was that nothing happened. Pop didn't speak, and I didn't speak. Not one single word. We cleared dishes and scrubbed pots, and Pop wouldn't even turn his face to me so I could see what was going on with him, what he was thinking. I didn't have the courage to ask and find out. But I felt as if I should say something.

We wiped tabletops and then the counters and everything was finally cleaned. I could escape to my bed.

Just as I was going in my room, I said, "I'll help you pack up tomorrow, okay?"

"Okay," Pop said.

And that was that.

21

ON SUNDAY, Pop and I carried boxes of stuff to the car. We always took the things with us that we really needed, like clothes and all, but other things, like dishes and pots that we got from Goodwill or the Salvation Army stores, we left behind us. Pop would never take more than would fit easily into the car. He said that was half the fun of moving, to go out and buy the stuff we needed, so we'd get it at garage sales and all. Only sometimes, we couldn't find what we wanted and we didn't have the money to get it new, so we'd do without. Like one whole year we lived without a toaster.

The entire time we packed, neither of us spoke. Usually we talk nonstop, but this time it was as if Pop was numb. Or dumb. He didn't seem angry, just kind of frozen maybe. I didn't feel as if I dared to speak. Maybe I felt numb, too, and I wanted to stay that way.

It was late Sunday by the time we finished. Pop left to go see Mr. Carneseca, our landlord, to get our deposit back and to tell him that he could keep whatever we left in the house. Pop felt bad about leaving Mr. Carneseca, I could tell. Mr. Carneseca is an old, old man, and lots of times he'd come around to the house just to talk and all. He always asked us if we wouldn't stay—we had a month to month rental, furniture and all. I don't know if he needed the money from the rent, or if he just liked Pop and me. But I know Pop liked him.

While Pop was gone, I wandered around the house, just looking. I went in the kitchen and my room and the little dining room, and the living room with Miss Holt's chair with the springs poking through the bottom.

Then I went outside and walked all the way around the house and then sat down on the porch steps. Going. We were really going away. It was really happening. Bailey. Brant. Miss Holt. Even this dumb old house would be gone. History, as Bailey would say. But still, I felt nothing but numb.

At least we'd tried.

I wondered if I should go and say good-bye to Bailey, but I didn't think I could. What if I couldn't find anything to say? Or worse, what if I cried? And anyway, she'd never told me exactly where she lived.

Maybe I should see Brant. He didn't even know yet. I hadn't told anyone but Bailey. But I couldn't see Brant. Not anybody.

Maybe later.

I got up off the steps and walked slowly toward school. That was dumb. Sunday and going to school. But I needed to see it one more time, too.

I found a can and began kicking it. It bumped along ahead of me, and I ran a few steps, catching up. Kick, run, kick, run.

Pop, why?

Kick.

Why, why, why?

Kick.

Again?

Kick.

Why don't you grow up?

Not fair, not fair, not fair. It wasn't fair even to think that. He was sad. It wasn't his fault that Mom had died, that he needed to move all the time.

Oh, hell.

Kick, run after it, almost to the steps of the school.

Someone was sitting on the corner of the school steps in our regular place, Bailey's and mine.

Bailey.

She was watching me, had probably watched me kick this stupid can all the way up the stupid street.

I gave the can a vicious kick out into the gutter. "What are you doing here?" I said. It came out meaner-sounding than I had wanted it to.

She shrugged. "Don't know."

"Oh."

I stood for a minute, then sat down beside her.

For a long time we sat not saying anything. After a while, Bailey dug into her jeans' pocket and took something out. A small piece of paper, folded over and over into a tiny square.

She handed it to me. "Read it later," she said. "I'm a lousy poet." She stood up.

I stood up, too. "Where are you going?" I said.

"Home."

"Can I. . . ."

She shook her head no.

"Well, how about. . . ."

152

"Unh, uh."

We stood there for a second, and then she took a little step closer to me. But then she stopped short, turned around, and ran away.

I watched her go, remembering the words I had heard in my head weeks ago, one of the first things I had thought about her: *That girl can run.*

Like a deer, she ran, or like a duck, skimming across the water as it's about to take off. Or like. . . . And then I said right out loud, "Please don't go." Even though I knew she couldn't hear me.

She was gone.

I unfolded the little scrap of paper and read:

> Jenny, the Lion, meets Seymour the Sam:
> Jenny, you know, once was a lamb.
> Now as a lion, she rules the North Sky,
> Then Seymour, the Sam, came by.
> Jenny and Seymour went playing in Rome,
> When suddenly Seymour had to go home,
> Home to his castle in the blue skies,
> And he left Jenny there with tears in her eyes.
> For Jenny, the Lion, though brave and bold, too,
> Can never replace the Sam who was you.

I sat down on the steps. Everything that had happened since Saturday began to well up in me. The planning. The dinner. Pop being mad at me. The silence. And leaving here and leaving Bailey.

Suddenly, I wasn't numb anymore. I began to cry, and I cried and cried. And I didn't care who saw me. I didn't even care if Bailey came back and saw me. I cried until I couldn't cry anymore. And when it was dark, I got up and walked home for the last time.

22

NEXT MORNING was Monday, and as everybody else was leaving for school, Pop and I were packing the last things into the car. Pop put the house keys in the dish in the garage for Mr. Carneseca, and we got into the car. Neither of us took even one last look after we pulled out of the driveway.

We still had hardly spoken since Saturday night. We hadn't said a word about Miss Holt and the dinner. I wondered if we'd drive all the way to Oklahoma like this.

I fiddled with the radio, just to have some noise, but even though Pop had fixed it—or tried to fix it—it was mostly static. Didn't matter. It was noise to fill up the silence, and I left it on.

As we went out of town, we went right by the school, but I didn't look. Pop was going to write to them for my records when we got where we were going, the way he always does, so we didn't have to stop. We went past all the stores—the A & P where Bailey and I had bought the stuff for dinner, the candy store where we jumped onto the roof. Past the museum she had wanted to explore at

Pop and I were packing the last things into the car.

night. Past the movies and McDonald's, and then past factories and gas stations, and then stuck in traffic. It had to be the worst time in the whole day to be going through the city.

I looked at my watch. Nine o'clock. School would be starting. I'd never even said good-bye to Brant. Would Bailey tell everyone I was gone for good?

What would school be like in Oklahoma? I'd have to make friends all over again, start all over. Had I gotten too old and grown-up for eating flies? It did get attention. Kevin Corbett eats flies. Five cents each. Ten cents for spiders. Swallows goldfish, too.

Would there be somebody like Bailey to say, "Chew it, Big Shot"? Would there?

Never.

I thought of the final line of her poem: "Can never replace the Sam who was you." I didn't know what a Seymour the Sam was. But I knew it was me, and I felt like crying again.

A couple of times, I noticed that Pop seemed as though he was about to say something, but then he'd stop. I didn't ask.

We must have driven for about an hour when the car began to slow. I looked at Pop. He was easing off to the side of the road, onto the shoulder. Did we have a flat? No, we weren't bumping.

When Pop had the car fully off the road, he put on the brake and turned off the ignition. He sat, not looking at me, but looking through the front window of the car. His face was really grim.

"What's the matter?" I asked. But I was afraid I already knew. He was finally going to tell me how angry he was, how disappointed in me.

That's all right. Better to get it over with. The silence all the way to Oklahoma would be too much.

"What?" I said again.

"I'm not sure I can do this," Pop said.

"Go ahead," I said. "I deserve it. Bailey and I were really stupid the other night. We did something stupid."

Pop shook his head the tiniest bit. "No, no," he said. "That's not what I mean. I don't think we can leave here."

"*Leave*?" I said. We were already leaving.

"This is no good," Pop said.

"What's no good?" I wanted to shout it. What was he talking about? Was he saying we were staying? I didn't dare believe that.

"You weren't stupid," Pop said. "You were just trying to make . . . I don't know . . . sense out of your life. Maybe put some sense into it." He tried to smile at me. "Or maybe into the old man." He shook his head. "Nah, I'm the one who's stupid."

"No, you're not," I said. "You're not."

"Yeah, I am." He turned to look at me. "Well, maybe not real stupid. But not grown up either." He was quiet for a while, and then he took a deep breath and said, "We're going back. I can get my job back. They were begging me to stay. Offered me a raise, even. And Mr. Carneseca, you know how much he wants us to stay. We'll move right back in. He said, 'Come back anytime.' He's going to be surprised how fast we take him up on that."

Pop was smiling, but suddenly there were tears in his eyes. He reached over and grabbed me, pulling me into his arms just the way he used to do when I was little. "I didn't know how much it meant to you," he said. "Till Saturday."

I felt tears flood my own eyes. I wanted to stay. More than anything in the world I wanted to stay. But it wasn't fair to Pop. It was terrible.

I pulled back out of his arms. "No," I said. "I think we should go."

"Can't." Pop's voice was firm. "We have to go back."

"But not for me!"

He laughed a little. "Partly for you. But for me, too." He turned to the window again and stared out. Cars whizzed past us on the highway, going . . . where? Were we really going to stay?

Pop put a hand across the back of the seat, then rested it on my head and sort of ruffled up my hair. He spoke, but he didn't sound like he was talking to me. "You know," he said, as if he were talking to someone outside the front window of the car. "You know, sooner or later . . . even grown-ups have to grow up.

"Let's go!" His voice was different—strong and clear. "Come on!" He turned on the ignition, then turned the car around in a big U turn.

As he did, all the static disappeared from the radio, and all the way back into town, music played as clearly as if the antenna was working perfectly normally.

"I'll drop you off at school," Pop said, as we came closer to town.

"Okay," I said. Any other day I'd have begged for a day off. But today I wanted to be there. To see Bailey. Brant. Maybe even it would be good to see Miss Holt. I wondered if she'd be mad about Saturday, though I didn't think so.

When we pulled up in front of school, Pop scribbled a note on a piece of paper saying I'd been sick earlier in the morning.

My heart was thumping hard against the center of my chest and my head was dizzy. Stay, stay, I was going to stay, not move again. Not move again! Always one more time, wasn't anymore. But I had to ask one more thing, even though I knew I shouldn't. I just had to.

"Pop?" I said.

He turned to me.

"Is this for good?" I asked.

Pop answered slowly, as though he knew that this was a time for honesty. "I'm not real sure. I think so. How about we just say for a good long while?"

I nodded. That was good enough. At least for now. Or at least for a good long while.

About the Author

PATRICIA HERMES had her first book for young readers published in 1980 and has written many more since then. Her books include *What If They Knew?*, recipient of the Crabbery Award, and *You Shouldn't Have to Say Goodbye,* winner of the Pine Tree Book Award. Both of these awards are selected by children. Three of her titles have been named Notable Children's Trade Books in the field of Social Studies by the National Council for the Social Studies-Children's Book Council Joint Committee. Her novels have been praised for their "vivid, painful believability" *(Bulletin of the Center for Children's Books)* and their "recognizable vitality" *(Kirkus Reviews).*

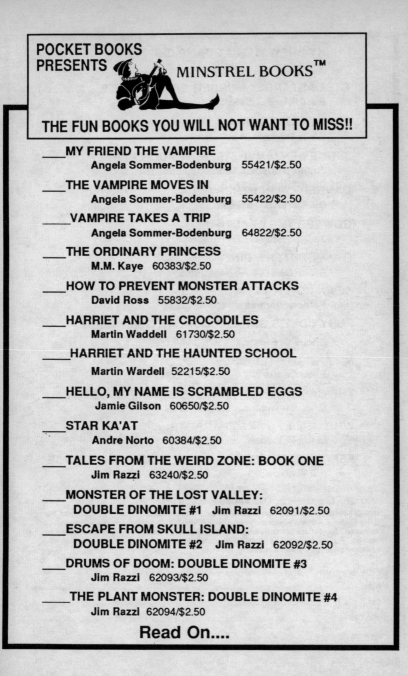

___**PUNKY BREWSTER AT CAMP CHIPMUNK**
  Ann Matthews 62729/$2.50

___**THE DASTARDLY MURDER OF DIRTY PETE**
  Eth Clifford 55835/$2.50

___**ME, MY GOAT, AND MY SISTER'S WEDDING**
  Stella Pevsner 66206/$2.75

___**JUDGE BENJAMIN: THE SUPERDOG RESCUE**
  Judith Whitelock McInerney 54202/$2.50

___**DANGER ON PANTHER PEAK**
  Bill Marshall 61282/$2.50

___**BOWSER THE BEAUTIFUL**
  Judith Hollands 63906/$2.50

___**THE MONSTER'S RING**
  Bruce Colville 64441/$2.50

___**KEVIN CORBETT EATS FLIES**
  Patricia Hermes 63790/$2.50

___**ROSY COLE'S GREAT AMERICAN GUILT CLUB**
  Sheila Greenwald 63794/$2.50

___**ME AND THE TERRIBLE TWO**
  Ellen Conford 63666/$2.50

___**THE CASE OF THE HORRIBLE SWAMP MONSTER**
  Drew Stevenson 62693/$2.50

___**WHO NEEDS A BRATTY BROTHER?**
  Linda Gondosh 62777/$2.50

___**FERRET IN THE BEDROOM, LIZARDS IN THE FRIDGE**
  Bill Wallace 63264/$2.50

200 Old Tappan Rd., Old Tappan, N.J. 07675

Please send me the books I have checked above. I am enclosing $_____ (please add 75¢ to cover postage and handling for each order. N.Y.S. and N.Y.C. residents please add appro-priate sales tax). Send check or money order--no cash or C.O.D.'s please. Allow up to six weeks for delivery. For purchases over $10.00 you may use VISA: card number, expiration date and customer signature must be included.

Name _____

Address _____

City _____ State/Zip _____

VISA Card No. _____ Exp. Date _____

Signature _____

724